Run for your Life

Wilma E. Alexander

Illustrations by Antonio de Thomasis

ROUSSAN
PUBLISHERS INC.
Specializing in YA and fiction for pre-teens

THE CANADA COUNCIL | LE CONSEIL DES ARTS
FOR THE ARTS | DU CANADA
SINCE 1957 | DEPUIS 1957

We acknowledge the support of the Canada
Council for the Arts for our publishing program.

We acknowledge the financial support of the Government
of Canada through the Book Publishing Industry
Development Program for publishing activities.

http://www.roussan.com

Copyright ©1998 by Wilma E. Alexander

National Library of Canada
Bibliothèque nationale du Québec

Canadian Cataloguing in Publication Data
Alexander, Wilma E., 1924-
Run for your Life
(An On time's wing book)

ISBN 1-896184-46-4

I. Title. II Series

PS8551.L473R86 1998   jC813'.54 C98-900973-4
PZ7.A54Ru 1998

Cover design by Dawn Lemieux
Cover and interior art by Antonio de Thomasis
Interior design by Jean Shepherd

Published simultaneously in Canada and the United States of America
Printed in Canada

2 3 4 5 6 7 8 9 AGMV-MRQ 4 3 2 1 0 9

To

Emily the Fair

with love

Preface

It was Thanksgiving Day, October 1918. The people of Trenton, Ontario were just sitting down to their dinner when a series of explosions rocked the small town, panicked the populace and broke the windows of every home.

The British Chemical plant, then the main industry in those days of World War I, blew up. The ammunition plant was gutted. People fled the town in panic by any means they could—horse, auto, wagon, bicycle, whatever was available. Those that remained in town gathered on the west side of Mount Pelion, hoping the mountain would shield them from the explosions.

Miraculously, no lives were lost. The war was over a few weeks later and the plant was never rebuilt. Vestiges of the cement foundations remain on the site, and people still tell tales of the explosion told to them by their elders.

The anxiety of being at war was not the only problem Canadians had to cope with. The Influenza Epidemic of 1918-19 was the most deadly influenza outbreak in history. It is said that 30 million people throughout the world died. Many schools and factories were closed in an effort to stem the spread of the disease. There were no modern preventative vaccines to fight the deadly virus.

CHAPTER ONE

"RUN! RUN FOR YOUR LIFE!"

She was running...over rocks, under trees, scrambling up the mountain, panting, trembling with fear. She had to reach the top. The blue and white bundle in her arms was heavy...so heavy. She wanted to put it down but didn't dare. The bundle wiggled and started to cry. Her feet slipped on loose gravel and she tumbled headlong through a pink haze.

Emily woke with a jerk. She wasn't holding a crying bundle. It was only her pillow clutched tight against her chest. She had been dreaming.

"Run for your life! Run!"

Emily sat up. Those screams were real. They came from the next room. Emily shook her mother's shoulder.

"Mama, Mama!"

Her mother struggled out of bed and into her old green kimono. "Go back to sleep, Emily. It's your aunt Carrie. I'll go to her."

Back to sleep, thought Emily. How could she? That terrible dream...and the screams. It was almost morning. In the grey light from the window she could see her father's picture on the dresser. He looked so handsome in his soldier's uniform. She missed him so much.

Emily heard her mother's voice, soothing and comforting. The screams changed to sobs. Emily slid down in bed and pulled the covers over her ears but she could still hear. She never got used to Aunt Carrie's spells.

She put her hand under her pillow and felt the cold smoothness of Muff, her little stoneware hot-water bottle. It was grey and shaped like a pig and had big blue spots. Emily ran her fingers over the tiny ears and snout.

He was cold now. The water in his hollow insides had cooled since she went to bed, but Emily didn't care. She always felt better when Muff was in her hand. It was Pa's last gift to her before he went away to war.

The sobs from the next room stopped and Emily drifted back to sleep. She woke when she heard the boarders going down to breakfast. Their heavy work boots thumped on the stairs. She listened to the rumble of their voices in the kitchen and the clattering of dishes as they ate their breakfast.

Emily took her time washing and dressing. She even made the bed. She didn't want to go down until the men had gone. They were big men with loud, rough voices. They made her feel very small but they were kind. One of them gave her a dime once.

She opened the bedroom window and leaned out to watch for the men to leave. It was a bright October day with frost sparkling on the grass. Her window looked out on Mount Pelion rising steeply from the end of the street. She leaned out further and craned her neck to the right.

Far up the river smoke hung over the munitions plant. The sharp smell of chemicals tingled her nose. Sometimes the haze drifted over the town like a veil and the smell was worse.

The milkman's horse and wagon turned the corner and Emily smiled and sighed. She should run down and give the horse a carrot. It was a day to be happy and she would be if only Pa were here.

Emily heard the door shut and saw two of the boarders leaving. They were carrying suitcases. What did that mean? She closed the window, gave her long, frizzy black hair a swipe with the brush and flew downstairs.

Her mother sat at the end of the table with her head in her hand surrounded by dirty breakfast dishes.

"Mama, what's wrong?"

Before she could answer, the other two boarders clattered down the stairs with their bags. They stood by the door, opening and closing their mouths and clutching their caps.

"We're real sorry, Ma'am, but we gotta leave," the shorter one finally blurted out.

"Can't get any sleep with all that yelling and groaning going on at night," said the other. "We're doing dangerous work at the munitions plant. Gotta have our sleep. Might blow ourselves up if we get careless."

Her mother nodded. She pressed her lips together and Emily knew she didn't want to cry in front of the men. She put her hands over her ears and closed her eyes. She didn't want to watch, she didn't want to hear.

"Here's what we owe you, Ma'am, and goodbye. It's been a good place to board." They clumped out and Emily put down her hands and opened her eyes.

Her mother was crying as she counted the handful of bills.

"Oh Emily, what are we going to do? Nobody will board here with your aunt Carrie the way she is. If only we could find her pay packet."

"We've looked and looked, Mama."

"It's got to be somewhere. She brought it home that dreadful day—her week's pay and the collection they'd taken up at the dairy for her wedding present.

"I'll have to find more boarders. There must be some workers who wouldn't mind Carrie's spells. Good boarding houses are scarce in Trenton now, with the war on and the munitions plant going full blast."

Emily spooned hot porridge from the big pot on the stove. "I'll look for the pay packet again when I come home from school, Mama."

Her mother hugged her. "Oh Emily, don't worry. I'll take in washing. Mrs. Howard has been after me to help her out ever since the new baby arrived. She has a pile of washing every day. Stop in on your way to school and tell her. That will be a big help."

Emily didn't want to stop at Mrs. Howard's. She was shy. But then there was the new baby. Emily loved babies. Maybe Mrs. Howard would let her look after him and she could earn some money to help Mama.

She went upstairs and took off the big apron she always wore over her school clothes. She couldn't decide whether to take Muff to school with her. It made her feel good to have the little muff pig in her skirt pocket where she could put her hand on him any time. But what if he fell out and broke? What if that terrible, horrible Dooley Smith chased her home again?

She put Muff under her pillow. He'd be safe there. She didn't want to take any chances with Muff.

There was no sign of Dooley all the way to school. Sometimes he didn't come on Friday, but he came in the afternoon, making faces at all the girls and teasing them at recess.

But for once Emily was not worried about Dooley.

There was something wrong with the teacher. Ever since recess Miss Sharp hadn't looked at the class once. Her face was flushed and her hands trembled. She gave them work to do, then put her head down on her arms. She hadn't looked up since.

It's the 'flu, thought Emily—the dreadful Spanish influenza that everyone feared. A lot of people even died from it.

Emily looked around the classroom. The other children sensed it too. They pretended to work but kept stealing looks at Miss Sharp and each other. Even Dooley, who never worked unless the teacher made him, pretended to be busy.

He looked up and made a horrible face at Emily. She shivered and looked at the schoolroom clock. The big hand was inching its way toward four. She put her books away. She had to be ready to go the minute the bell rang. If she hurried she would be first out the door and Dooley wouldn't see which way she went.

Should she go home the long way, by the sidewalk, or take the shortcut over the mountain? It was steep and rough but shorter.

The bell rang and Miss Sharp stood up, trembling and swaying. "Class dismissed." She stopped Emily as she tried to rush past.

"Emily, please clean the blackboard and do Monday's date. I...have to leave." She didn't wait for an answer.

"Yes, Miss Sharp." Emily groaned inside. She wanted to get out fast, but maybe if she dawdled over the job Dooley would be gone.

She picked up the felt eraser and cleaned the black slate in long back and forth swipes. Emily liked doing things after school. If only Dooley didn't make life miserable for her. She had enough things to worry about without him.

Being little was one of her problems. She dragged a chair over to do the top of the board. Almost ten, Emily was the tiniest person in the class. She couldn't do anything about Dooley or Pa or Aunt Carrie or the missing money. There was nothing she could do about anything.

Emily chose coloured chalks for the date—yellow for the day—Monday; orange for the month—October 7th; green for the year—1918.

It looked pretty and for a moment she felt happy. Then her shoulders sagged. October 7th, 1918. Pa had been gone for a whole year now. He was far across the sea, fighting in the trenches. She was so afraid for him. Sometimes she felt she couldn't stand one more day without him. If only a letter would come. There had been no letter in a long time.

She put her hand in her pocket to feel for Muff. Then she remembered. He was still under her pillow. She closed her eyes and thought of Pa's words the day he left. He had wrapped her fingers around the little stone pig.

"There, Emily. Every time you fill this little muff pig with hot water, think of me and be brave. When I come back I'll buy you a beautiful velvet muff. Then when you go walking in the winter this little pig will keep your hands toasty warm."

Emily opened her eyes. It was time to go home. She brushed the chalk dust off her navy-blue skirt and pulled up her long black stockings. They always sagged at the knees. She grabbed her jacket from the cloakroom and went down the long hall to the big double doors. She poked her head out and looked around.

No sign of Dooley. She would go over the mountain. Then she would be home sooner to see if Mama had been to the Post Office.

Emily hurried across the playground at the back of the school and took the path leading up the mountain. She didn't stop to admire the coloured leaves as she usually did. Her eyes darted from side to side. You never knew with Dooley. He was apt to jump out from anywhere.

"Run, Em'ly. Run!"

Emily stood rooted to the spot. Her heart felt as if it would jump right out of her chest. Terrified, she looked around. There he was, halfway up a tall maple tree, leering down at her.

He bared his big white teeth in a terrible grin and pulled his black hair over his face.

"I've been waiting for you, Em'ly."

CHAPTER TWO

Emily forced her feet to move and took off as fast as her skinny legs would go. When she was almost to the top of the mountain she looked over her shoulder.

Dooley was big and heavy and it was taking him time to climb down the tree. She would never make it down the other side of the mountain, but she might have time to hide!

On the crest of the mountain an old iron cannon pointed out toward the Bay of Quinte. Emily hurried to the grassy verge and wiggled under the barrel of the cannon. She put her hands over her mouth and tried to be very still. Her heart pounded. Would Dooley hear?

In a few seconds he arrived at the top. Emily heard him gasping for breath. For a moment the wind in the trees was the only other sound, then... "You can't hide from me Em'ly Rogers. I'm going to find you wherever you are!"

Emily crouched under the cannon. Why couldn't Dooley leave her alone? He was always chasing kids, but he seemed to pick on her. He couldn't even say her name right. He always left out the *i*. Then she heard his footsteps going away.

She waited a bit then jumped up and headed for the path down the other side. It was steep and choked with brambles. She should go slowly and carefully but she was afraid of Dooley.

Too late! She tripped over a rock and went head first down through the bushes, ending up at the bottom. Her hands and face were scratched and bleeding. There was a hole in the knee of her stocking. She put her head on her knees and started to cry. Nothing was right and it wasn't fair.

"I see you Em'ly. Here I come!"

Dooley! He had followed her down. She couldn't run any more. Her chest hurt and her legs felt like rubber, but she had to try. Her shabby, white clapboard house was only half a block away.

Emily picked herself up and ran. She could see Aunt Carrie wrapped up in shawls, sitting on the porch in the rocking chair. Could she make it? Dooley was close behind. She could hear him puffing.

Up the steps, past Aunt Carrie, around the corner of the house. She couldn't go a step further. She flattened herself against the wall, taking deep, gulping breaths, then she poked her head around the corner.

Dooley was charging up the steps. Then he saw Aunt Carrie. She rose from her chair, trailing shawls, and stared past him with blazing blue eyes. Her big white straw hat trimmed with pink roses and lengths of white lace fell to the floor. Dooley stopped dead.

"Beware the place of death." Her voice hissed and she pointed up the river with her long white finger.

"It is evil. Run, you are doomed."

Dooley's face went as white as paper. He tried to back down the steps but tripped and rolled to the sidewalk. He picked himself up and caught sight of Emily.

"You and your loony aunt," he shouted, shaking his fist at her. "Your whole family's crazy, Em'ly, and you too. Afraid of your own shadow."

He sauntered down the street whistling to show he wasn't afraid, but the whistle was thin and he broke into a run at the end of the block.

Emily shivered and almost laughed. It should be funny to see Dooley Smith, the school bully, run away scared but she was too frightened to laugh. Dooley was right. She was afraid—of everything and everybody. She was even afraid of Aunt Carrie.

Emily felt ashamed of that. Aunt Carrie used to take

her to the ice-cream parlour for treats. They sat on fancy wire chairs at little round marble tables and ate banana splits and told jokes.

But that was before her aunt's dreadful trouble...before she became this strange creature that no one understood.

She peered around the corner again. Her aunt was calm now, staring up the river, tears spilling down her face. She was a strange sight, standing there in a pale yellow summer dress with a pile of shawls at her feet. Her bright red hair was piled in a bun on top of her head, making her look even taller. Emily took her by the hand.

"Come, Auntie, come into the house now. You're cold."

"No, no." She sat down in the rocking chair. "I must wait here. He'll come soon and I won't be ready. Where's my hat?"

"Here it is." Emily picked up the big hat and put it in her lap. She tried to drape the shawls around her, but Aunt Carrie pushed her away and began sewing on the hat. She poked the needle in and out as fast as she could.

"It will soon be finished," she muttered, "and then I'll be ready."

Emily left her and went around the house to the kitchen door. Steam rose from a huge wooden tub in the middle of the floor. The sharp smell of laundry soap and bleach almost made her sneeze. Her mother hadn't wasted any time. She was ironing and folding clothes into a big basket.

"There you are, Emily. I need you to deliver Mrs. Howard's wash. I'll lift the basket into the wagon for you. Don't take all day. I want you to start supper when you get back. I have to do more laundry tonight."

She put the iron down and looked closely at Emily. "What's wrong? You look pale. Aren't you feeling well?"

Emily heard the fear in her voice. She's afraid I'm getting the 'flu, she thought.

"And where did you get those scratches on your face? And look at the dirt on your blouse. I hoped it would do one more day. How did you get that hole in your stocking? Emily Rogers, what have you been up to?"

"I'm all right, Mama. I fell coming down the mountain path. Dooley chased me home again."

Mrs. Rogers shook her head and went back to her ironing. "You have to learn to stand up to that boy, Emily. He just chases you because you run. Try standing still next time and see what happens."

"Oh no. I couldn't do that." Emily shuddered at the thought.

Her mother shrugged. "Well you'll just have to put up with it then. I've got my hands full with Carrie and the washing and worrying about your father. Did I hear her shouting out there. Is she having another wild spell?"

Emily tried to brush the dirt off her blouse and pulled

her skirt down to hide the hole in her stocking. "She's all right now. She's working on her hat."

"She's been trimming and retrimming that hat for weeks now. At least it keeps her busy. Wash your face and hands before you go out. Can't have you on the street looking like a tramp."

Emily splashed water on her face and hands then got the wagon from the shed. Her mother lifted the laundry basket into it, and Emily tiptoed past the veranda so Aunt Carrie wouldn't notice her. At the end of the walk she stopped and looked up and down the street. Dooley might be lurking somewhere.

There was no one around except two little girls across the street raking leaves. They waved. "Hello, Emily. Come and play. We're making leaf houses."

Emily shook her head. "Have to deliver this washing."

The girls giggled. "Too bad. I'm glad we don't have to do that," said the bigger one. "I'd rather play in the leaves."

So would I, thought Emily. At the next brick house she rang the doorbell.

"Well if it isn't our Emily," said Mrs. Howard when she opened the door. She was fat and full of smiles. "Wait until I get my basket."

Emily tiptoed over to the big wicker baby carriage on the porch. The newest Howard baby, Alex, was asleep, bundled in a white blanket with blue rabbits on it.

Emily wanted to pick him up and hug him, but she didn't dare. She put her hand on his cheek. It was warm and soft, like velvet.

When Mrs. Howard came out with her laundry basket, Emily helped her fill it with the clean clothes. "Could I mind the baby some day, Mrs. Howard?" It took all her courage to ask.

"Land sakes no, Emily. You're much too little. He's a big boy and you might drop him."

Emily hung her head and her face went red. Why had she ever asked? She knew she could hold him. She was strong.

Mrs. Howard carried the basket down the steps to the wagon. "That's a big load for a wee mite like you. Pity you ain't tall like your ma. You've got her frizzy black hair and big brown eyes though. Here's your money. Better put it in your middy pocket so you don't lose it. Your ma needs it. Ever find Carrie's missing pay packet?"

Emily shook her head.

"Too bad about that. Guess you could use it with your pa overseas and all."

Emily started down the walk—glad to get away from Mrs. Howard.

"Here, hold on, Emily. I got something for you."

Emily waited and squirmed. Why did she have to mention her hair. She hated it. It was black and frizzy like her mother's, but at least her mother could pile hers on top of her head in lovely coils.

Emily's long hair was just like a bush, bouncing up and down against her back when she ran. She'd been running a lot lately. When her mother put a ribbon in it the bow practically took off like a bird. She could hardly wait until she was sixteen and could put her hair up.

Mrs. Howard came back and put a book into her hand. "Here, Emily. My sister sent this for my Ruby but she ain't one for books. You might as well get some good out of it, seeing as you're so crazy about reading. It's one of those Elsie books."

Emily smiled and forgave her everything. "Thank you, Mrs. Howard, thank you." She was glad Ruby didn't like to read. Ruby was only two years older than Emily, but she was tall and did everything right. She never fell down and tore her stockings or muddied her middy blouse. But then Dooley never chased her either. Ruby had long smooth hair the colour of corn silk, and it curled down to her waist in long sausage curls.

"Oh, oh!" Mrs. Howard stared past Emily at the house across the street. A boy wearing a smart navy-blue uniform with red piping got off his bicycle and went up to the door. He carried a yellow envelope in his hand. It was the boy from the telegraph office.

"Oh dear God, that poor woman!" Mrs. Howard waddled down the steps and started across the street.

Emily stood frozen to the sidewalk. She knew what a

telegram meant. It meant bad news. It meant someone had been killed in the war.

She made her feet move and tore down the street as fast as she could, faster even than if Dooley Smith was chasing her. The laundry basket bumped up and down in the wagon and almost fell off. What if the boy had two telegrams to deliver? What if he had already been to their house? What if Pa had been killed?

No!...No!...she screamed inside herself. No. Pa can't be dead. He can't be.

CHAPTER THREE

B<small>Y THE TIME</small> E<small>MILY</small> reached the house, she had a pain in her chest. She left the wagon by the back steps and put her hand on the doorknob.

She couldn't go in. She didn't want to go in and face the news. But she couldn't stand there forever. She had to know. Her hands trembled so she could barely turn the knob. She sidled in and leaned against the door.

Her mother stood over the steaming tub, scrubbing clothes on the washboard. She looked the same. Emily slumped against the door and sobbed in relief. Nothing had happened.

"Emily? What's wrong?" Her mother raised her head and stared at her. "Dooley Smith been chasing you again?"

Emily gulped. "I...I saw the telegraph boy. I thought he'd been here." Her tears overflowed.

"Oh, Emily." Beth Rogers took her daughter's hands and pulled her over to the couch. "It's all right. There hasn't been a telegram."

She laughed and squeezed Emily's hands. "Look, I've got your hands all wet and soapy. Here, I'll dry them on my apron and let's wipe away those tears." She hugged Emily and rocked her back and forth.

"There'll be a letter soon. I know there will be. Then we'll know he's safe. Now I have to get back to my washing. You bring in the basket and put the wagon away. Then you can start supper."

Emily nodded. She went out to put the wagon in the old stable. No horse had lived in it since her father went away to war, but it still smelled of horses and hay and straw. Maybe when her father came back from the war, they could have a horse and buggy.

She closed her eyes and imagined what it would be like. She'd be prancing down Front Street with her parents in a shiny black buggy with a fine horse to match. She would wear a starched white dress with a cherry-coloured sash and hair ribbon to match. Or maybe in winter they'd have a red sleigh and bells and she'd have her cherry-red velvet muff with Muff-pig tucked inside. And she'd stick out her tongue at Dooley—

"Emily!" her mother called from the doorway. "I'm

making some tea. Bring your aunt Carrie."

Dragging her feet Emily walked to the front porch and stood in front of her aunt. "Aunt Carrie?"

No answer. Her aunt kept on sewing furiously at her hat. She jabbed the needle in and out of the fine yellow veiling as if she were stabbing an enemy. Emily didn't know how she could see. It was nearly dark.

Emily took the hat from her and put it on the table.

"Auntie, come and have a cup of tea. It's ready."

No answer. Emily took her arm. She hated to touch Aunt Carrie since she had gone all strange. Once she had given her hundreds of hugs but not now.

"Come Auntie, a cup of tea will do you good."

Her aunt sat like a statue. Emily went back into the house. "She won't come, Mama."

Her mother shook her head. "I don't know what we're going to do with her when winter comes. She'll freeze to death sitting on that porch. I'll just have to drag her in."

Emily got out the knives and forks. She could hear her mother scolding, and Aunt Carrie crying. In a few minutes they came in, her mother pulling her sister by the arm.

"Emily, go out and bring in her things."

Emily went out and gathered up the shawls and sewing things. She looked up the river toward the sprawling munitions plant. It had changed the life of Trenton. It had changed Aunt Carrie, too, from a beautiful, happy young woman into a weird, sad creature.

Then she remembered she hadn't looked for the pay packet. It was too dark now. Emily looked over the porch rail. Something moved in the bushes.

"Who's there?" she quavered.

There was no reply. A shadowy figure scuttled out of the bushes along the sidewalk and ran down the street. Emily was sure it was Dooley Smith.

Why was he hiding there? She shivered and ran back into the house.

After supper Emily did the dishes while her mother finished the wash. "I'll hang the clothes out to dry in the morning," she said. "I'm so tired. You take your aunt Carrie into the parlour and play the phonograph. The music soothes her and maybe she'll be quiet until bedtime. You can mend that hole in your stocking, too. I'm going to write to your father."

Emily opened the lid of the rosewood phonograph and turned the crank on the side until it was tight.

She switched on the turntable and gently lowered the arm holding the needle. Pa said they must be careful not to scratch the records.

Aunt Carrie rocked back and forth and hummed along. Emily hunched over her stocking, pulling the edges of the hole together with black wool. If Dooley hadn't chased her she wouldn't have to do this. It was all his fault. She'd rather be reading her new Elsie book.

When the record ended her mother came in. "I'm taking Carrie up to bed now. Maybe we'll have a quiet night for a change. Finish your stocking, then off to bed."

She put her letter beside Emily. "You might write a few words to your father. He'd like to hear from you."

Emily stared at the letter then picked up the pencil. *Dear Pa, I miss you.* Then she could think of nothing more to say. *I love you. Emily.*

Up in the bedroom she took Muff from under her pillow. She stopped to look at Pa's picture. If only the war would stop, and he could come home. Nothing had been right since he left. She wanted things to be the same as before.

Pa had worked at the hardware store and Aunt Carrie at the dairy. Emily had her own room and Mama looked after them all. Then everything changed.

Tears came but she brushed them away. She wasn't going to cry. Pa said they all had to be brave and she seemed to be crying all the time.

She took Muff down to the kitchen and filled him with hot water from the reservoir in the stove. She stroked his warm back and cuddled him against her cheek.

Then Emily noticed her aunt's sewing things on the kitchen table. The hat wasn't there. It must still be out on the porch. It would be all right until morning. She didn't want to go out. It was dark and Dooley might be there.

She started up the stairs then stopped. Maybe Dooley

would steal the hat for a joke or because he was mean. Maybe the wind would blow it away. If it disappeared Aunt Carrie would really go crazy. She had better go out and get the hat.

Emily put Muff in her pocket but kept her hand on him for comfort. She opened the door and walked slowly along the dark porch.

Slam! Emily jumped and turned. Then breathed again. It was only the wind slamming the kitchen door shut. At top speed she tore around the corner of the house, grabbed the hat, and was back in the kitchen in a flash. She leaned against the door until she got her breath back. It was silly to be so afraid, but she couldn't help it.

Back in the bedroom Emily laid Muff on her pillow and got ready for bed. Then she knelt and said her prayers. "And God bless Pa and keep him safe," she whispered.

Muff had warmed her pillow. She tucked him under her chin and closed her eyes.

The next day was Saturday. The river sparkled in the sunlight and the munitions plant didn't smell too bad. Emily longed to take her new book and Muff and climb the mountain. She wanted to sit astride the cannon and enjoy the sun and the autumn colours, but she couldn't. It was her job to dust and help her mother on Saturdays.

She was afraid to go up the mountain anyway. Dooley Smith might be up there.

Mama settled Aunt Carrie on the porch with her shawls and hat and sewing basket. "That hat has so many flowers and veils and ribbons it must weigh two pounds. It will be too heavy to put on her head. Oh well, it keeps her busy."

Emily followed her mother back to the kitchen and got the dust cloth.

"Emily, leave the dusting and help me hang out the wash. In this sun it will dry by noon. I'll iron it and you can deliver it before supper."

They went out to the backyard and Emily handed her mother a long white petticoat to hang on the line.

"Emily!"

Her mother dropped the pegs. The petticoat fell over Emily's head. She yanked it away and looked around to see what had startled her mother.

She was standing at the peeling white picket fence that surrounded the yard. Her hands gripped the pickets so hard her knuckles showed white.

"Mama, what's wrong?"

Beth Rogers didn't answer. She stared up the street, her tall figure rigid against the fence. Emily saw two men walking toward them. One was slightly bent and limped. He looked familiar.

CHAPTER FOUR

Emily's heart jumped. "Pa?" She could barely whisper the word. Then she knew it wasn't Pa at all—only someone who looked like him. She took her mother's arm.

"Come on, Mama. It isn't Pa."

Her mother sagged as if the life had gone out of her. She turned back to the clothesline. "I know, Emily. I was foolish to hope."

Emily looked back. The two men were looking over the fence.

"Look. Those men. They've stopped here."

Her mother gave a little cry. She ran toward the taller man and took his hand.

"Bert...oh Bert. I thought you were..."

The man patted her hand. "I know, Beth, I know. You

thought I was Dave."

Emily looked at him carefully. He was tall like her pa, with the same sandy hair, grey eyes and freckles. His face was thinner and he was stooped. Deep lines marked his face and his eyes were sad. He limped and didn't look strong enough to carry his heavy suitcase.

He really wasn't like Pa at all, she thought. Pa's grey eyes were always laughing. He was big and strong and could scoop her up in his arms and toss her in the air with no trouble at all.

"You must be Emily." The man looked down at her and smiled. "You look like your ma, only littler. I'm your uncle Bert and this is your cousin Tom."

Emily squinted up at the boy standing behind his father. The sun was in her eyes and she could see only a thin figure—all arms and legs and almost as tall as Uncle Bert. He put down his bundles and moved toward them.

"Hello, Aunt Beth. Hello, Emily."

Her mother grabbed him in a big hug. "Tom, little Tom. I can't believe it's you."

Tom's freckled face went red right up to the blond cowlick that scooped across his forehead. "Guess I'm bigger now."

"Bigger? You're all grown up. Come right in and tell me what you're doing in Trenton."

She opened the gate for them, then looked back at the basket of wet clothes.

"Oh dear. I have to get that wash hung out. Emily, take your uncle Bert and Tom into the kitchen and put the kettle on the stove. We'll have a cup of tea and a nice visit. It's good to see you, Bert."

Her uncle smiled and his long sad face lit up. "It's good to see you, Beth. Tom will finish hanging out the wash for you. Emily can help and see that he does it right. I need to talk to you, Beth."

Emily looked at her mother. She didn't want to be left to help this strange cousin hang out the washing. She wouldn't know what to say to him. She didn't want to be alone with them in the kitchen either. She never knew what to say to people she didn't know.

Behind her Tom sighed. He stood there frowning and digging his heel into the grass. He doesn't want to do it either, thought Emily, feeling sorry for him.

"Jump to it, Tom," his father said.

Tom put the bundles on the back porch and headed toward the clothesline. Her mother nodded at her so Emily followed.

He picked up the petticoat her mother had dropped and draped it over the line far above Emily's head.

"Got any clothes pegs?" he said, holding out his hand but not looking at her.

She picked up the cloth bag and handed him one of the wooden pegs. They worked silently for a few minutes.

He knows how to do this, Emily thought. She forgot

that she was shy and smiled up at him.

"You've done this before."

"Lots of times. Since Ma died I've learned to do a lot of things. Dad doesn't think I do them right though." He looked straight at Emily for the first time.

"You tell him, will you?" His eyes pleaded with her.

"Tell him what?"

"That I hung out the wash and did it right. If I don't do things exactly the way Ma did, he says it isn't right. Can't see what the difference is...long as things get done. Can you?"

Emily nodded. But she knew she could never go up to that strange uncle and tell him that Tom knew how to hang out washing. She was too shy.

She couldn't say no to Tom either. He was the first person who'd ever asked her a favour. Most people didn't notice her very much.

They went into the house to find the two parents sitting at the kitchen table. The big brown teapot steamed in the centre and there was a plateful of lemon cookies.

Her mother was smiling. She looked happier than she had for a long time.

"Your uncle Bert is going to work at the munitions plant and board with us. Tom can go to school with you."

She squeezed Tom's hand. "It will be good to have you both. I'm worried about you working at the plant, Bert. Explosives are so dangerous. Dave used to say the whole town would blow up some day."

Uncle Bert shook his head. "Maybe it will and maybe it won't, but I need a job and it pays thirty-five cents an hour. Can't beat that anywhere. Can't run the farm since I hurt my foot, and with Lucy gone it just isn't the same. Tom and I've been knocking round all over the place."

Her mother started pouring the tea. "Emily, go out and bring in your aunt Carrie. She hasn't seen Bert and Tom in a long time. Seeing them might help her."

"Ma, you know she won't come for me."

"Try, Emily. Maybe Tom will help."

Emily led Tom out to the long porch that almost circled the house. Aunt Carrie sat at the far end, facing up the river toward the munitions plant. She was sewing long lengths of yellow veiling to the broad straw hat.

Emily stood in front of her, twisting her hands in her apron.

"Aunt Carrie. Ma says you're to come in. Tea's ready."

Her aunt didn't move. She stared past Emily. "Is he coming yet? My hat isn't ready. I'll have to hurry. Can't be married in any old hat."

Tom stared and brushed his hair out of his eyes.

"What's she talking about? Is she getting married soon?"

Emily shook her head. She didn't like to talk about her aunt to anyone, but Tom was a relative.

"She and Robert Lott were to be married last August.

He worked at the munitions plant. Aunt Carrie worked at the dairy. On her last day they took up a collection for her wedding present. She came home and put her pay packet with the wedding money in it on that table."

Emily pointed to a small wooden table shaped like a cloverleaf.

"Then she sat down to finish trimming her wedding hat and wait for Robert to come down the street from the plant. She was so proud of all the money she had for their wedding."

Emily stopped. Tears crept down her cheeks. She didn't like to remember that dreadful day.

Tom picked up the corner of her apron and tried to wipe her tears away. "Don't cry, Emily."

Emily cried harder. Pa used to wipe away her tears.

Tom lost patience. "Emily, hurry up and tell me the rest of the story. Your ma's waiting and I'm hungry."

Emily gulped and tried to talk through her sobs. "Well, there was a big bang and then the siren went. That's the signal of trouble at the plant. Some men came and told Aunt Carrie that Robert Lott had been killed. She's never been the same since."

Emily picked up the big summer hat and wound the veiling around it. "All she does is sit out here and sew on this hat and wait for Robert to come. We haven't seen the pay packet since."

Tom took Aunt Carrie's hand. "Aunt Carrie. Tea's

ready. Won't you come in and have some?" He smiled into her eyes.

Aunt Carrie stood up and put her hat on top of her sewing basket. "Yes, thank you. Who are you, young man? Are you a friend of Robert's?"

Emily watched with her mouth open.

"I'm Tom," he said then offered her his arm. She took it and Tom walked her to the kitchen.

Emily shook her head and followed. "He's magic," she muttered.

The next day was Sunday and Tom and Emily and her mother walked up the road by the river to the small North Trenton church. Uncle Bert stayed home to watch Aunt Carrie.

The sermon was long and Emily got tired sitting on the hard wooden pew. She started to wriggle and dropped her hymn book. Everyone turned to see what the crash was. The minister stopped talking and frowned. Her mother scolded, "Emily!"

Emily's face got red and she covered her face with her hands. She wanted the floor to open and swallow her. Tears dribbled between her fingers.

Tom poked her. "Look!"

He took a big, grimy white handkerchief out of his pocket and made it into a rabbit that wiggled its ears at her.

Emily tried not to giggle. She forgot how embarrassed

she was and watched Tom make the rabbit do tricks. Before she knew it the sermon was over, and they were outside waiting while her mother visited with the neighbours.

On the way home she scolded Emily for dropping the hymn book.

Tom laughed. "You're just a butterfingers, Emily."

Her mother turned on him. "Now don't you talk, Tom Rogers—making rabbits in church, indeed. And that dreadful, dirty old handkerchief. Don't you know enough to take a clean handkerchief to church?"

"Only one I've got, Aunt Beth." Tom grinned and poked Emily. "Race you home."

"Not on Sunday, young man," her mother answered for her. "You put that handkerchief in the wash as soon as you get home. Your father will have to buy you some more. One handkerchief isn't enough."

Emily smiled. Life was going to be more interesting with Tom around.

Monday morning Emily could hardly wait to take Tom to school with her. Let Dooley try chasing her now. She had Tom to protect her. He was taller than Dooley.

Uncle Bert finished his breakfast and went off to the munitions plant. Tom was taking forever to eat his. He had two bowls of porridge, two pieces of toast and jam and three glasses of milk. Emily stood at the door with her coat on.

"Come on, Tom. We'll be late."

Tom looked around the table. "I'm still hungry, Emily. Is there any porridge left, Aunt Beth?"

"It's all gone, Tom," her mother said with a smile. "But you and Emily may each take an apple. I'll have dinner ready when you come home at noon."

They started down the street in the October sunshine. Tom grabbed her apple and tossed it up in the air with his, doing a fine juggling act. Emily laughed. "If you drop them they'll squash, Tom."

"Don't worry. I can juggle." He pretended to drop one, catching it just before it hit the sidewalk.

Emily laughed. She felt almost happy. She waved at Mrs. Howard who was putting the baby out to sleep on the porch but she kept a sharp eye out for Dooley. He was nowhere in sight.

"The school is on the other side of the mountain," she explained to Tom. "We'll go around it now by the sidewalk and come home over the top by the path."

"Mountain? What mountain?"

Emily grabbed his arm and pulled him around. "That mountain." She pointed to the tall hill on their right.

Tom snorted. "Go on. You call that a mountain? I've seen hills bigger than that."

Emily's eyes filled with tears. "It is too a mountain.

Everybody around here calls it the mountain."

"Emily. Don't cry. You're like a fountain. Hey, that rhymes with mountain! Sorry if I hurt your feelings. If you want it to be a mountain then it is. Doesn't make any difference to me."

Tom looked back at the mountain and shook his head.

Emily wiped her tears and said nothing more. The joy had gone out of the morning. She hated people making fun of the things she loved. She wasn't like a fountain. Or was she?

I do cry a lot she thought, but I can't help it. She had hoped Tom would be her friend.

He strode on ahead, munching one of the apples. Emily had to run to keep up. They reached the tall red brick school at the foot of the mountain with Emily panting for breath.

No one was playing on the swings or the slide. The children were all gathered around the big double doors of the school.

"It can't be true," said one of the older girls.

"It must be," said another. They were looking at a large sign nailed to the door.

Emily and Tom were at the back of the crowd so she couldn't see. "What's wrong? What's on the sign? Why are the doors closed? Can you see?" Emily pulled at Tom's sleeve.

Tom pushed closer. SCHOOL CLOSED, he read. BY

ORDER OF THE TRENTON BOARD OF HEALTH THIS SCHOOL IS CLOSED UNTIL FURTHER NOTICE DUE TO THE INFLUENZA EPIDEMIC. He stumbled over the last words but everyone knew what it meant.

Some of the children cheered and some groaned. Emily's heart sank. She liked school. It took her mind off Pa being away and Aunt Carrie and everything else.

She heard shrieks and saw three little girls chasing Dooley up the street. He was laughing that terrible laugh and waving a girl's hat. Emily shivered. Then she remembered. She had Tom now. She wouldn't have to worry about Dooley anymore.

"Too bad you can't go to school, Tom."

Tom was still staring at the sign. He grinned. "Doesn't hurt my feelings. I can find lots to do. Might even get a job. If I eat a lot and grow a lot I could join the army. I'd like to be a soldier."

"They wouldn't take you. You're too young."

"I'll be old enough some day. Hope the war lasts until then." He finished his own apple and started eating hers.

Emily stared at him. How could he hope for such a thing? She wanted the war to end, soon, so her pa could come home.

"Well, if the war doesn't get you the 'flu might," she said. "Mrs. Howard says it's real bad. People dropping like flies, she says."

Tom laughed. "We won't let any germs catch us,

Emily. Come on, I'll race you to the top of your mountain. I want to see what's up there."

He bounded toward the path and Emily followed. She knew she'd never catch up to his long legs so she took her time. She was tired of running. When she reached the top, Tom was already sitting astride the cannon looking out toward the bay.

Emily climbed up in front of him and pointed to the river winding through the town into the bay. "That's the Trent River and that's the Bay of Quinte. Teacher says the great French explorer Samuel de Champlain stood on this very spot hundreds of years ago."

Tom took off his cap and let the breeze blow his hair. "If I'd been Champlain I'd have stayed right here. I like it up here. You can see a long way."

Emily felt good. This was her favourite spot. When she sat on top of the cannon, she felt she owned the whole world and nothing could ever go wrong. She was glad Tom liked it too.

He slid off the cannon and crouched under the long barrel to look at the base. Emily heard feet pounding up the path. It was Dooley.

He made a horrible face and snarled. "Run, Em'ly, run. Here I come. I'm going to get you!"

CHAPTER FIVE

EMILY CLUNG TO THE cannon. She thought she was going to faint.

Then Dooley's mouth fell open and his eyes bulged out. He stared past Emily.

Tom was standing up, leaning against the barrel.

"You are going to do what?" Tom's voice was snarly too.

Dooley gulped. "Who are you?" He began to back away.

Tom moved toward him. "I'm Emily's cousin. You'd better leave her alone." Tom took another step.

Dooley ran.

Emily laughed until she fell off the cannon into the tall grass.

"Oh Tom, I'll never forget his face when you rose up behind the cannon. You scared him silly."

"For now," said Tom. "He's shorter than I am but he's a lot stronger. He'd win in a fight."

"Oh no, Tom. You could beat him."

Tom shook his head and broke off some of the tall grasses. He leaned back against the cannon and started braiding the grasses.

"Why does Dooley chase you?"

"I don't know." Emily watched his quick fingers. "He just does. He always chases me home."

"Does he chase you any other time?"

"No, just when I'm going home. What are you making, Tom?"

"Hmm. You know Emily, I don't think Dooley would bother you if you stood up to him."

"What do you mean?"

"Well, the next time he says he's going to get you, just stand pat and don't run. Bullies always back off if you stand up to them."

Emily was horrified. "Oh I couldn't do that. I'm too scared. Anyway you're here now, Tom. I don't need to."

"You should look after yourself, Emily. I won't always be around."

He grabbed Emily's arm and tied the braided grasses around her wrist.

"There. Now every time you feel afraid of Dooley, look

at this bracelet and remember what I said. Stand up to him."

Emily looked at the bracelet. The grasses were different shades of green and brown. It was pretty.

"I'll try, Tom. Thank you."

Tom frowned. "Maybe I should take that bracelet back," he said. "I asked you to do me a favour but you didn't."

Emily put her arm behind her back. "What?"

"I asked you to tell Dad that I hung out the clothes right."

Emily hung her head. "I just couldn't, Tom."

"You must admire your boots an awful lot, Emily. You're always staring at them."

Emily's face burned and angry tears stung her eyes. She glared up at Tom. He put up his hand.

"Whoa! Now don't start crying again, I'm only teasing. Glad to see you've got some spirit though." Tom grinned. "Come on, I'll race you home. It must be dinnertime. I'm hungry."

"After two apples," Emily shouted but he only waved and plunged down the hill.

Emily ran after him. She wasn't going to stay up on the mountain alone. Dooley might be hiding, waiting for Tom to leave. She was going to tell Uncle Bert what a good job Tom had done hanging out the clothes, even if it killed her.

Her mother was surprised to see them home early.

"There may be no school for you two, but don't think you can go larking around all day. I've got lots of work you can do. Busy hands don't get into mischief." Her voice was cross but her eyes twinkled.

Emily looked at Tom. She didn't usually get into mischief and she was sure Tom didn't either—well—maybe just a little. He had a saucy glint in his eye.

Tom winked at her. "Sure Aunt Beth, what's to do?"

"You and Emily can do the dinner dishes, while I finish up the wash and hang it out. Then you can chop some kindling, while Emily chops the vegetables. I want to make chili sauce today."

Emily's mouth watered. Her mother made the best chili sauce in the whole of Trenton.

"I can hang out the washing if you want," said Tom.

"No, I need to get out in the fresh air. I'm feeling poorly today."

Emily perked up her ears. Her mother was never sick. But then it was a beautiful autumn day. Who wouldn't want to be outdoors?

Doing dishes had never been such fun. She washed and Tom dried and kept her laughing. He picked up a plate and bowed to it.

"Will you have this waltz with me, Mrs. Plate?"

Then he danced it around the room. "Oh pardon me, Mrs. Plate, you have some soap suds in your eye! And some on your back! Let me give you a wipe."

By the time he waltzed back to Emily the plate was dried and he was ready for another. Emily laughed so hard that tears filled her eyes.

Tom pretended to be cross. "What? Crying again? I'm going to call you Miss Fountain! We'll be having a flood if you don't stop."

By supper time the chili sauce was made and the washing was dried and ironed. Emily helped her mother get supper and Tom set the table. When Uncle Bert came home from the munitions plant, he sniffed and a big smile lit up his sad face.

"Long time since I smelled chili sauce acookin'. Tom's ma made the best there ever was."

Beth Rogers tossed her head. "I think you'll be able to choke mine down. Come now, everyone sit around the table and let's eat. When you and Tom are finished, Emily, you can deliver the wash to Mrs. Howard."

Emily could hardly eat her supper. She had to tell Uncle Bert how well Tom did things. Tom had scared Dooley away. He'd made her a beautiful grass bracelet and he made washing dishes fun. Now it was her turn to do something for him.

"Uncle Bert."

Everyone looked at her. That is what she hated—

everyone looking at her as if they were amazed that she had spoken. Emily stared down at her lap.

Tom kicked her under the table. "Can't stare at your boots now, Miss Fountain," he whispered.

That made her so mad she plunged right in. "Uncle Bert, Tom did a good job hanging out the wash the day you came and he can dry dishes better than me!"

It all tumbled out at once and everybody laughed. Emily's face got red and she covered her face with her apron.

Uncle Bert pulled the apron down and his eyes twinkled for a change. "He'll do, Emily, and you're a fine lass to stand up for him."

When supper was finished Tom loaded the wash basket on the wagon and Emily led the way down the street. Tom pulled the wagon. As they trudged along in the dark he squeezed Emily's shoulder.

"Thanks, Emily. For what you said back there. That was good. Nobody ever stood up for me before except Ma, and she's dead."

Emily smiled. It was nice to have a cousin who was a friend. Maybe she wouldn't miss Pa so much now that she had Tom.

They reached the house and stood on the street, looking in the window of Mrs. Howard's parlour. A young girl was practising the piano. The light from the lamp shone on her long, fair sausage curls, turning them to gold. She wore a pink dress and a pink hair ribbon. Her hands were like white butterflies, hovering over the keys.

Tom stared and Emily heard him gasp.

"Who's that?"

"It's Ruby Howard. You'd be in her class if school wasn't closed."

Tom gulped. "She's beautiful."

"Yes, she is," Emily muttered, feeling small and plain.

Tom started up the walk. "Come on. Let's take the laundry in. Maybe she'll come to the door."

Emily stood still. She didn't want to stand beside the beautiful Ruby.

"You go ahead. I'll wait here. Don't forget to collect the money."

She hoped Tom would insist that she come but he didn't. He grabbed the basket of laundry as if it weighed nothing at all and bounded up the steps and rang the bell. Emily saw him smooth back his hair and brush off his knee breeches while he waited.

She turned and ran home. She wasn't going to wait and watch. Tom could talk to Ruby all he wanted. It was none of her business. She wasn't going to let Ruby see her standing all alone on the sidewalk like a ninny.

Her mother was waiting at the door. "Where's Tom? Where's the wagon? Did you get the money?"

"He's coming with the money." Emily bent over and

yanked up her stockings. She didn't want her mother to see her face.

"Why didn't you wait for him? It's not very nice to leave him to come home all by himself. He doesn't know a soul in this town."

He does now, thought Emily. She didn't tell her mother that Tom was probably making friends with Ruby Howard right now.

She went up to her room and looked in the mirror. Her hair was all bushy and little wisps hung down over her red, sweaty face. Her middy blouse had spots on it and her stocking wrinkled around her ankles. Her hands were dirty and her hair ribbon sagged over one ear.

"I am not beautiful," she said to the face in the mirror. She twisted the grass bracelet on her wrist. Would Tom make a bracelet for Ruby too? No. Ruby wouldn't want a bracelet made of grass. She would want real silver and gold.

Emily yanked the bracelet off and shoved it under a pile of handkerchiefs in her drawer. Then she pulled Muff from under pillow, tucked him under her chin and had a good cry.

Soon she heard Tom's voice in the kitchen. She didn't want to go down and hear all about the beautiful Ruby Howard, but it was cold in her room and it was too early to go to bed. Emily splashed cold water on her face and shoved Muff in the pocket of her skirt. Then she picked up her Elsie book and went down to the kitchen, trying to look as if she didn't care a pin about Tom or anybody else.

Uncle Bert was playing records on the phonograph for Aunt Carrie and trying to get her to talk. But she sat staring into space and never answered. Maybe we'll have a quiet night tonight, thought Emily. Her mother was darning a sock by the lamp, and Tom sat on the floor with the checkerboard on his lap.

"Want to play checkers, Emily?"

"No thank you." Emily hoped she sounded frosty.

"Aw c'mon. What else are you going to do?"

"I'm going to read." Emily opened the book and held it in front of her face though she wasn't reading a word.

"Dad? Aunt Beth? Aunt Carrie?" Tom looked from one to the other.

They all shook their heads except Aunt Carrie who looked straight through him as if he wasn't there.

"All right. I'll play with Jack, then."

"Jack? Who's Jack?" Emily couldn't help asking.

"He's my imaginary pal. He's always there when no one else will play with me." Tom set out the checkers on the board. "You take the black ones, Jack, and I'll have the red. All ready?"

Emily giggled. Tom was so funny. All her hurt disappeared. She put down her book and plopped down in front of the board.

"My move first."

Tom pretended to frown. "Well now, I don't know, Emily, I promised Jack but...What's that, Jack? You have to go home? Well that's too bad. Come again. Bye. You're on, Emily."

They played three games. Emily won one but she suspected Tom let her win. It was fun but soon it was bedtime and she took Muff to the kitchen to fill him up with hot water.

Tom watched as she dipped water from the reservoir. "That's some pig, Emily. Where'd you get him?"

"Pa gave him to me. Before he went overseas."

"He's awful small to be a bed warmer."

"He's a muff pig. My grandmother carried him in her muff a long time ago. He's my friend."

"That's a funny friend."

"Not as funny as your friend Jack." Emily was surprised at herself. She didn't usually answer back.

Tom laughed. "You're right. At least you can see your friend."

When her mother came up to bed, Emily was reading with Muff tucked underneath her chin. Her mother sat down on the side of the bed and started rubbing her hands with goose grease.

Emily covered her nose with the blanket.

Her mother smiled. "I know you don't like the smell of this, Emily, but it's the only thing that keeps my hands from chapping. They're in water so much."

"Never mind, Mama, when Pa comes back from the war you won't have to take in washing any more."

"We'll see, Emily. Now we must go to sleep. I think I'm getting a cold."

Her mother put the lid back on the jar and turned out the light. The bright October moon made silvery paths on the floor. Soon, oh make it soon that Pa comes home, Emily prayed. We need him so much. Then she had a thought.

"Mama, could you do my hair in sausage curls?"

"No, dear. You haven't got the right kind of hair. Now go to sleep."

The next morning was cold. Frost covered the grass and the red and yellow leaves. Emily shivered as she dressed. It would soon be Thanksgiving, then Hallowe'en, then Christmas. Oh, if only Pa could be home for Christmas.

Down in the kitchen her mother put Emily's porridge in front of her, then sat down to cough.

"What's wrong, Mama? Is your cold worse?"

"It seems to have gone to my chest." She coughed again. "We're all out of cough syrup...you...can go to the drugstore and get some...oh, my chest hurts...then stop at the Post Office for the mail."

Emily stared at her mother's face. It was red with fever and there were dark circles under her eyes. A little flutter of fear ran over her. Not the 'flu. Not Mama, too.

She grabbed her jacket, stuck Muff in her pocket, pulled her old blue tam over her ears and ran all the way to the drugstore. She was in such a hurry that she forgot to put on her woollen gloves. Her fingers were stiff with cold by the time she got there.

The druggist wrapped up a bottle of cough medicine for her. Then she climbed the steps of the old stone Post Office and joined the line at the wicket. When it was her turn she stood on tiptoe and put her face close to the brass grille.

"Mail for Mrs. Rogers on Front Street, or Miss Emily Rogers, please?"

The man behind the grille sorted some letters. "Nothing today, Emily. Guess you haven't heard from your pa for a while?"

"No." Emily could barely manage a thank you. She went outside and stood on the steps. She knew she was going to cry. Tom could call her a fountain all he liked, but there were some times she just had to cry and this was one of them.

She wished she could go up the mountain, curl up under the cannon with Muff and let the tears flow. But she couldn't. Mama needed the cough syrup.

Emily rubbed her wet cheeks with her hand and started home. She could taste the salt tears on her lips. She tried to lick them away as fast as they ran down her face. It was awfully uncomfortable crying in the cold wind, and she had forgotten her handkerchief. She curled her cold fingers around Muff in one pocket of her jacket and around the bottle of cough syrup in the other. There was no warmth in either one.

She turned the corner on to Front Street and saw someone dart back into the doorway of the hardware store. Emily stopped. It was Dooley. He must have been hiding there all ready to jump out at her as she passed. She pretended to stop and look in a store window. What would she do now?

She thought of what Tom had said. "He only chases you because you run. Stand up to him."

If only she could. Then she remembered the grass bracelet Tom had made for her. He said it was magic and would help her stand up to Dooley. Emily felt her wrist. It wasn't there! She had torn off the grass circlet when she was mad at Tom for admiring Ruby.

There was only one thing left to do. She crossed the street and started to run.

"Run, Em'ly, run!"

The crazy laugh and taunting words pursued her down the street. Legs pounding, gasping for breath, Emily ran as if a pack of hungry tigers were after her. There was no time to cry. She needed all her energy to keep ahead of Dooley.

One block to go! She sobbed in relief as her house came

in sight. Dooley was getting closer. If only she could reach the porch. Aunt Carrie was sitting there and Dooley was afraid of her. She crossed the leaf-covered lawn. She was almost at the porch when her feet slipped on the wet leaves. Down she went, head first.

She rolled over and saw Dooley standing over her, his lips pulled back in a terrible grin.

"I've got you now, Em'ly Rogers."

CHAPTER SIX

ANGER SURGED THROUGH HER. She was tired of running, tired of being picked on. "No you haven't, Dooley Smith!" she shouted and kicked at his ankles.

Dooley's mouth dropped open and he staggered, trying to keep his balance. Emily jumped up and ran into the house. She was shaking but she felt good. She looked out the window and saw Dooley standing in the leaves staring at the house with a surprised look on his face.

She had done it. She'd stood up to Dooley Smith. Where was Mama? She had to tell her, and Tom too.

The kitchen was empty and so was the rest of the downstairs. Then Emily heard a cough from upstairs. She ran up to the bedroom.

"Mama, I did it, I..."

Her mother lay on the bed coughing and coughing. Her face was scarlet and shiny with sweat. She raised one hand and let it fall again when she saw Emily.

"Mama! What's wrong? Is your cough worse? I brought the medicine."

Emily pulled the bottle from her pocket and went back to the kitchen for a spoon. Her hands shook as she poured out a dose for her mother.

"Emily, I'm sick." Beth Rogers coughed again. "You'll have to look after things...I'm weak."

"Oh, Mama. I can't." Emily's voice trembled. "You'll be better soon. The medicine will make you better."

Her mother closed her eyes. She fell back on the pillow and didn't answer. Emily covered her with the quilt and went back downstairs. Her mother would be better after a good sleep. Mama couldn't be sick. She'd never been sick before. What would they all do?

Emily looked at the clock. It was nearly dinnertime and she was hungry. Uncle Bert was at the munitions plant and there was no sign of Tom. Who would get dinner and how could she get Aunt Carrie to come in and eat? She would have to try.

There were some cold potatoes and ham in the pantry. She'd fry the potatoes and cook some carrots to go with them but the fire in the stove was almost out. The wood box was empty. She went out to the woodshed to get more from the tall pile against the wall. Tom was there chopping kindling wood. Emily felt better at once.

"Oh Tom, Mama's sick and it's dinnertime and the fire's almost out and what'll we do?" Tears filled her eyes but she didn't try to stop them.

For once Tom didn't tease her about crying.

"Come on, Emily. Let's get that fire going and have something to eat, then we can figure out what to do." He gathered up an armful of wood. "Bring some of that kindling in."

Emily gathered up the slim sticks and followed him back into the house.

Tom soon had the fire going and between them they made a meal. When it was ready Emily went upstairs to see if her mother felt better, and Tom fetched Aunt Carrie from the porch. She was shivering and her hands were blue with cold, but she sat at the table and ate what was put in front of her.

"Mama won't come down, Tom. She doesn't want anything but a cup of tea."

"She'll be all right. Probably needs a good rest. We can manage until she's better. Eat your dinner, now. I'll make the tea and you can take it up."

But Emily couldn't eat. The food tasted like flannel. Mama hadn't even asked if there was a letter from Pa. She must be really sick!

Uncle Bert came home, put his hand on Mama's forehead and sent Tom for the doctor. It was late at night when he came, looking old and tired. He looked at Mama and shook his head.

"Spanish 'flu. Town's full of it. Can't even get you a nurse. They're all on cases."

"We can manage." Uncle Bert's face looked grim. "My wife died of the 'flu some time ago."

"You know what to do then. Keep her warm, give her the cough medicine and try to keep her strength up. Beef broth's good."

He snapped his bag shut and put on his coat. "Got three more calls to do before I see my bed. Goodnight. Call me if there's any change."

Emily felt like crying again but there weren't any tears left. She helped Uncle Bert put up a cot in her mother's room so Mama could have the bed to herself. Then she looked for Muff. Where was her muff pig?

She remembered he was in her pocket when she went for Mama's medicine. Emily went down to the kitchen. Uncle Bert was in the rocker by the stove, puffing on his pipe.

"Forget something, Emily?"

"I left Muff in my coat pocket." Emily went to her coat hanging on the row of hooks by the door. She put her hand in one pocket then the other. Both were empty.

"He's gone! Muff's gone!"

"Must be around somewhere. Where'd you last see it?"

"In my pocket...when I went for Mama's medicine. Dooley chased me home and I fell and..."

She reached for her coat. "He's outside. I've got to find him."

"Hold on," said her uncle putting his pipe down. "It's a dark night. I'll get the lantern and give you a hand."

They went out and Emily tried to remember exactly where she'd fallen. They kicked the leaves aside and Emily searched the piles of cold, wet leaves, but Muff was not to be found.

"Have to wait 'til morning, Emily...too dark to see an elephant, much less a little stone pig." Uncle Bert blew out the lantern and they went back into the house.

Emily felt the world had come to an end. What else could happen? She couldn't sleep a wink without Muff under her pillow, but she was so tired. She was asleep the moment she pulled the quilts up to her chin.

For the rest of the week Emily didn't have time to worry about Pa, or Muff, or Dooley, or anything else. Uncle Bert helped as much as he could but he had to work at the munitions factory.

Emily and Tom looked after Mama and Aunt Carrie and the meals. She told Mrs. Howard that her mother couldn't do the washing. Mrs. Howard understood. She sent a jar of beef broth for Mama.

She hardly had time to miss Muff. Each night she fell into bed so tired that she was asleep at once. She even forgot to say goodnight to Pa's picture.

At first Mama was delirious at night and woke Emily with her cries. Emily settled her down with sips of broth and covered her up, then fell instantly back to sleep.

Some nights Aunt Carrie cried out too. "Doom, doom. We are all doomed. Run for your life!" But Tom heard her and soothed her back to bed. She liked Tom and sometimes looked right at him, not through him as she did most people.

By Saturday, Mama was better. The fever was down, but she still had the cough and was so weak she could hardly raise her arms.

"The worst is over now," said Uncle Bert. "She just needs lots of rest and some good food."

Emily looked at the calendar on the kitchen wall. "It's Thanksgiving on Monday. I forgot all about it."

Uncle Bert reached in his pocket. "Here Emily, you and Tom go to the butcher's and see what you can get for a Thanksgiving dinner. We'll celebrate. They tell me turkeys are scarce but see if you can find one."

Emily put the money carefully in her pocket and she and Tom went shopping. They bought the last turkey in the butcher shop along with stew meat and sausages.

Outside the shop they met Mrs. Howard and Ruby. Ruby was pushing her little brother's carriage. Her long, golden ringlets shone in the sun. She smiled at Tom and ignored Emily.

Mrs. Howard beamed. "Morning Tom, morning Emily. How's the sick?"

"Oh, she's much better. Her fever's down and she's eating a little." Emily tried not to watch Tom and Ruby.

"Well, you take good care of her, you hear? I've known some to be getting better and go out and get a chill and die the next day." She snapped her plump fingers. "Just like that!"

Emily shuddered and looked at Tom. He was beaming at Ruby but he'd heard. He grabbed Emily's arm and pulled her away.

"Oh, we'll take good care of her. Never fear. Good day."

He pushed one of the parcels into Emily's arms as they walked along the street. "Here, I can't carry everything," he growled. "Silly old woman. Can't keep her mouth shut. Don't you fret, Emily. Your mama's going to be all right."

He stopped and looked into her face. "You're not going to cry are you?"

Emily shook her head. She wasn't going to cry in front of Tom. She'd never seen Ruby cry.

Mama managed to eat a bit of the stew on Sunday, and Uncle Bert helped Tom and Emily get the Thanksgiving turkey ready.

"We'll put it in the oven first thing Monday morning and have it for dinner. I have to go to work right after.

We're working short shifts because of the holiday. Tom can help you clear away. He's good at it."

Tom beamed. "Don't worry, Dad, we'll be fine."

Thanksgiving Day was grey with a drizzling rain. Just the way I feel, thought Emily, as she hurried to get dressed and look after her mother. But there was no time to think about her feelings. She and Tom and Uncle Bert were busy all morning getting the Thanksgiving dinner ready.

"Mama said she might try to come down and sit at the table for dinner," Emily told Uncle Bert at breakfast.

"I don't know. She's pretty weak but we'll see," he said. "Tom, maybe you could get Carrie to help us. She could peel potatoes."

They all looked at the tall, beautiful woman. She was wrapping herself in shawls to go out on the porch.

"Aunt Carrie," Tom smiled his best smile. "Would you help us with the Thanksgiving dinner this morning?"

She didn't look at them but she spoke. "Oh no. I have to finish my hat. I'm being married on Saturday you know." She picked up her hat and her sewing box and started for the door.

Emily tried to hold her back. "But Aunt Carrie, it's a wet day. You'll be cold and damp on the porch. Why don't you work on your hat right here. You can sit by the stove and be all warm and cosy while you sew."

Her aunt pulled away. "I have to watch for Robert. He'll be so happy when he sees the money they gave me at the dairy. Maybe we'll buy a phonograph for our new home." She went out and Emily started after her.

"Let her go," said Uncle Bert. "She'll get better in her own time. We'll just have to humour her until then. Losing someone you love is an awful shock."

His face sagged and Emily knew he was thinking of his wife.

Tom stoked up the wood stove and Emily made the dressing for the turkey, running upstairs every few minutes to ask her mother what to do. Uncle Bert helped her stuff the turkey and put it in the oven. Tom peeled the potatoes and carrots, while Emily tidied up the house and got the good dishes from the china cabinet.

Then she spread the white linen tablecloth Mama saved for company. She set the table, stopping to admire the gold rims on the best china. When she was all finished Emily looked at it. Something was missing. The table needed decorations to show it was Thanksgiving. Coloured leaves would do.

Emily looked out the window at the rain drizzling over everything. She threw her mother's old shawl over her head and went out into the yard. The leaves were sodden with rain and stuck together, but she gathered the prettiest and rolled them in her apron. She kept hoping she'd find Muff but he wasn't there.

Aunt Carrie huddled in her chair on the porch. She wasn't sewing. Her hat was on her head. She gazed up the river toward the munitions plant with sad eyes.

Emily looked upriver too. A yellowish haze hung over the hills that hid the plant, and the sharp sulphur smell burned her nose.

She unrolled her apron. "Look Aunt Carrie. I'm going to decorate the table with these leaves. Aren't they pretty?"

Her aunt didn't turn her head. She continued to stare. "When is Robert going to come? He's late today. He'll be so pleased about the money. Is he coming now?"

Her voice sounded far away. Emily shivered and looked up the street. She knew Robert would never come along that street again, but she couldn't help looking when Aunt Carrie asked. When was she going to admit that he was dead?

Emily put the leaves in the warming oven to dry for a while, then scattered them on the table.

"Looks real pretty, Emily," said Tom. "A real Thanksgiving table. When do we eat? I'm hungry."

"You're always hungry, Tom," his father said. "Now let's get this meal on the table. Emily you go up and get your mother ready, then Tom and I'll help her down."

Emily helped her mother into her green flannel robe and brushed her hair. Then Tom and Uncle Bert half-carried her down the stairs and propped her up with a pillow in the armchair at the head of the table.

Tom went out to get Aunt Carrie, while Uncle Bert carved the turkey. Soon they were all ready to begin.

Uncle Bert bowed his head. "We will all give thanks," he said. "You're first, Emily. What are you thankful for?"

Emily didn't know what to say. Pa was away at war, Muff was lost. Then she looked down the table at Mama, pale and weak and thin. "I'm thankful Mama is getting better," she said.

Uncle Bert nodded. "And you, Carrie, what are you thankful for?" No one expected an answer but she blurted out one word. "Robert," she said.

There was silence for a moment, then Uncle Bert nodded and looked at his sister-in-law. "And you, Beth?"

"Just to be alive," she whispered.

Tom was next. "I'm thankful for this Thanksgiving dinner. I'll be even more thankful when we can start eating!"

They all laughed and his father said, "I'll make mine short then." He looked around the table. "I'm thankful to be part of a family again. Let's eat."

Emily thought it was the best dinner she had eaten in a long time. If only Pa could have shared it too. Her mother tasted a tiny bit of everything but was soon too tired to sit up any longer. She was put back to bed and Emily promised to save her a piece of pumpkin pie.

"Tom made it, Mama, so I don't know what it will be like," she warned.

After dinner Uncle Bert went to work, and Tom and Emily cleared away the food and did the dishes. Emily wanted to go up the mountain when the work was done. She hadn't perched on the cannon since Mama got the 'flu. There hadn't been time.

She looked out the window but it was still drizzling. The path would be muddy and slippery. She would have to wait for a nicer day. It wouldn't be the same without Muff either.

Tom challenged her to a game of checkers, and they played and listened to the phonograph until it was almost dark.

"I'm hungry," announced Tom.

"After all the food you ate? And two pieces of pie?" Emily teased.

"Well it was good—even if I did make it."

"We'll have leftovers. I'll take Mama some broth, and you bring Aunt Carrie in."

But Aunt Carrie refused to come in, even for Tom.

"I'll take her out a turkey sandwich," said Emily. "She'll have to come in soon. It will be too dark to sew."

They made themselves plates of leftover turkey and dressing and bread and butter and sat at the kitchen table with a pot of tea between them. Emily felt very grown-up and put only a little milk in her tea.

73

"Best turkey I ever ate," said Tom between mouthfuls.

"You said it was the first time you ever—"

A long shrill whistle split the air and tore at their eardrums.

"What was that?" Tom had a turkey sandwich halfway to his mouth.

Emily turned pale. "It's the whistle at the plant. It means something's wrong. An accident."

Tom stared at her with wide eyes. "Pa," he whispered.

Then a siren began a long eerie wail. Emily put her hands over her ears and closed her eyes. Why was the siren going? What did it mean? The old feeling of fear and helplessness swept over her.

Tom stood up. "Pa's there. I've got to—"

A tremendous blast shook the whole house. Emily opened her eyes to see Tom flying through the air. The woodshed door burst open and Tom disappeared.

CHAPTER SEVEN

Emily grabbed the edge of the table. Her body was being forced against it. It was as if a giant hand was squeezing the breath out of her. Everything went black but she could still hear.

All around her the house shook. Dishes rattled and crashed to the floor. Something banged across the roof. Upstairs there was a deafening thud.

She opened her eyes. She was under the table and the lights were out. The kitchen door stood wide open. An eerie pink light picked out shards of glass littering the floor.

She crouched there for a few seconds, her heart pounding. Where was Tom? She had seen him flying through the air as the blast tore through the house. What had happened? Carefully she inched her way out from under the table and stood up. The kitchen was a shambles but she couldn't worry about that now. She had to find Tom.

He was not in the kitchen. Emily looked at the wood-shed door hanging from one hinge and leaning crazily across the opening. There was barely room for her to squeeze under at the bottom. She poked her head through and her heart almost stopped. The outside shed door was torn off too, and in the strange pink light from the doorway she saw Tom lying on his face in a pile of shavings.

She knelt beside him and managed to roll him over. Tom groaned and Emily went weak with relief. He wasn't dead but there was blood on his face.

"Don't move, Tom. I'm here. I'll help you. Just lie still."

Tom groaned again and put his hands to his face. He was still holding the turkey sandwich.

Emily crawled back into the kitchen. The stove had shifted and the stovepipe had come apart, spilling soot everywhere. The towel rack lay split in two pieces over the warming oven. She grabbed a tea towel and wet it.

Tom was still where she had found him. Gently she wiped his face. He groaned and opened his eyes.

"Emily! What happened?" He moved and groaned again. "Who hit me? Where am I?"

"Hush. We're in the woodshed. Something blew up. Your face is cut and there's a big bruise on your cheek. Is anything broken?"

Tom sat up slowly. "I don't think so. My head hurts, and my shoulder. I feel awful stiff..."

He looked at the sandwich still in his hand. "Where'd this come from?"

"You had it in your hand when..."

Tom popped it in his mouth. "Might as well finish it." He choked and stared past Emily through the doorway. "Gosh! Look at that."

The strange pink haze swirled outside. The sky was a lurid red. There was a spooky stillness in the air. Nothing stirred. He grabbed Emily's shoulder.

"It's the munitions plant! It's blown up!"

"Mama!" Emily shouted and dived back into the kitchen and up the stairs. Tom was right behind her.

The door to her bedroom was wide open and still on its hinges. Her hairbrush and Pa's picture and other things from the dresser were strewn about. Her mother's bed lay flattened on the floor. She was curled up on it, weeping, and huddling the quilts around her.

Emily put her arms around her. "Oh Mama, it's all right. We're here. We're all safe. Tom thinks the plant blew up."

Her mother struggled to sit up. "Carrie. Where's Carrie...and Bert," she gasped.

Emily looked at Tom. He didn't say a word but clattered back down the stairs.

"Come on, Mama. We've got to get you dressed. I don't know what's going to happen next."

Emily helped her mother into as many warm clothes as she could pile on her. By the time she had finished, her mother was weak from the effort. She lay down again on the collapsed bed. Emily covered her with the quilts and went down to find Tom.

She found him on the porch. Aunt Carrie's chair and her little table were overturned. The things from her sewing basket were scattered across the floor, and a piece of yellow veiling was wound around the railing.

Tom stood looking toward the blazing plant, holding Aunt Carrie's wedding hat in his hand.

"She's not here, Emily. I've looked all around but she's not here." He stared up the river toward the munitions plant. Masses of flames leapt hundreds of feet in the air.

"She kept warning us you know. And we didn't pay any attention. Oh Pa!"

Tom's head drooped and he dug his fists into his eyes.

Emily didn't know what to do. Tom usually comforted her but now it was her turn. The thing was to keep him busy. She took the hat and pulled at his arm.

"Tom, come on. We've got to find Aunt Carrie. Oh, oh, look at the chimney."

They stared up at the roof. What was left of the

chimney tilted dangerously and bricks were scattered all over the roof.

At that moment another explosion sent them staggering against the fence. They watched in horror as a great column of fire spurted up from the plant site. Bits of burning debris landed in the yard and fizzled out in the fine rain that still fell.

"Come on," yelled Tom, grabbing her hand. "We've got to get inside."

Tom ran to the stove. The fire had gone out. Emily reached for a stick of wood but Tom stopped her.

"We can't light a fire. The stove pipes are all pulled apart and the chimney's down."

"But Mama has to be warm."

"Maybe we can take her somewhere," said Tom. "Let's find out." He ran outside.

Emily was still holding Aunt Carrie's hat. She ran into the parlour and put it on the phonograph. Some of the ceiling plaster had come down. The pictures on the walls were crooked, but there wasn't much damage. She ran outside to join Tom.

People were hurrying by, pushing carts filled with their belongings. Some hadn't bothered with coats. Two cars filled with people drove carelessly through the crowds, honking their horns. People clung to the running boards and others tried to climb on the luggage racks at the rear of the cars.

Tom stopped a man pushing a wheelbarrow with a suitcase and a big kitchen clock in it.

"Where's everybody going?"

"We're gettin' out o' town, lad. Trenton's going to blow up any minute now. You'd better run for your life."

He went on, dodging in and out among the panic-stricken crowd.

"Oh Tom. What'll we do?"

"I've got an idea. Get your mother downstairs and bring a pillow and as many blankets as you can. And hurry!"

He ran up the street and Emily went up to her mother. First she took the quilts and the pillow off her mother's bed and flung them over the banister into the hall below. Then she put her arm around her mother.

"Come on, Mama. We have to go downstairs now. The plant blew up. We have to leave."

"I'm too weak, Emily. I can't walk. You go on. Where's Carrie and Tom?" Her mother sagged against her arm.

"He's gone for help, Mama. Come on. Try to stand up."

Emily staggered under her mother's weight, but they managed to get to the top of the stairs. They sat down on the top step and worked their way down, one step at a time. At the bottom Emily left her mother to rest and ran outside.

Tom was at the gate. He was holding the reins of a bony grey horse, harnessed to an old cart.

"Tom. Who owns that horse? You didn't steal him, did you?"

"No, I borrowed him. Stop asking questions and get Aunt Beth out here."

"You'll have to help, Tom. I could hardly get her down the stairs."

Tom shook his head. "Can't. If I leave this rig somebody will commandeer it. Everybody's gone crazy trying to get out of town. Can't blame them. All that dynamite and guncotton at the plant is making lots of bangs!"

Emily ran back to the house and brought out the bedding. Tom was helping Mrs. Jackson from across the street and her three little ones into the cart.

"I'm giving them a lift," he explained. A siren wailed in the distance and another burst of flame lit the sky. "Hurry, Emily."

Emily never knew how she did it, but she got her mother out of the house and Tom helped her into the wagon. The neighbour made a bed for her at the back among all her bundles.

Tom tossed the reins to Mrs. Jackson. "All right, Emily. Up you get and away you go."

"Aren't you coming?"

"I have to find my father. Hurry up, Emily. There might be another blast any minute."

Emily stood her ground. "I'm not going anywhere, Tom Rogers. I have to look for Aunt Carrie." Her voice shook.

Tom looked disgusted. He tossed his hair out of his eyes and gritted his teeth.

"I'll do that. You go on. I've told Mrs. Jackson how to get to our farm at Wooler, and I gave her the key to the house. You should be safe there."

Emily stamped her foot. "I've told you. I'm not going. Mama will never forgive me if I don't find Aunt Carrie." She reached up and slapped the horse's rump.

"Giddy up," she shouted. The cart jolted off and the little ones waved as they joined the stream of people headed out of town.

Tom stared after them with his mouth open. "Emily, you do beat all. You're not even crying."

Emily was surprised herself. She usually cried when things went wrong. And where did she get the grit to stand up to Tom? She had changed since she defied Dooley Smith and she liked it.

"There isn't time to cry. Where do we look first?"

Tom pointed up the river toward the fiery sky. "He's there. Somewhere. I'm going to find him."

They started down the street toward the bridge. The street was a river of people. They caught up with Ruby Howard, pushing the baby carriage loaded high with bundles. Her lovely golden hair was dull and tangled.

Her face was stiff with fear, and she stared straight ahead of her, bumping people out of her way.

Behind her Mrs. Howard waddled, her arms filled with bundles, tears running down her face.

Ruby didn't speak but her mother managed to pant a few words. "Oh, Emily," she puffed, "what's to become of us? We'll all die for sure. Thank God Ruby's got the baby...I'll never keep up." She stopped to catch her breath.

Emily stopped beside her. "Where are you going, Mrs. Howard? Have you seen Aunt Carrie?"

The woman wiped her face with one of her parcels. "Land no. Gone has she? We're going to the other side of the mountain up behind the school. They say it will be safe there. If I see Carrie I'll hang on to her...Ruby, wait. Wait for me!"

Mrs. Howard pushed ahead but Emily stood still, thinking, letting the stream of people flow around her. Did Ruby really have the baby in that carriage? It had been filled right to the top of the hood with bags and bundles. If the baby was under there, he didn't have space to breathe.

Maybe he was still back at the house. Maybe, in the panic, they hadn't noticed he was not in the carriage. No, that was crazy. Mrs. Howard would never forget her own baby. But Ruby might. She was scatterbrained.

Another explosion blasted through the sky, sending

up brilliant shafts of coloured fire. The crowd screamed and groaned and jostled Emily along. She was too small to resist them and was carried along the street for a few blocks. Mrs. Howard and Ruby disappeared from view.

She managed to work her way into the doorway of the hardware store and crouched there, out of breath. She had to go back to the Howard house. The baby might be there. All alone, with no one to look after him.

Tom was lost in the crowd so she was on her own. Keeping close to the walls she headed back, stepping over glass from the shop windows and piles of burning debris.

It took her a long time to struggle the two blocks back to the Howard house. She had to push against the crowd frantic to get as far away as they could from the deadly munitions plant.

She reached it at last and sank down on the steps to catch her breath. Then she knew she'd been right. A baby was crying in the empty house.

CHAPTER EIGHT

THE FRONT DOOR WAS locked but the big front window
had shattered. Emily climbed through the gaping hole,
tearing the sleeve of her jacket.

The baby was in the kitchen, on the couch. He was
wailing and waving his arms and legs. He stopped when
he saw Emily. She gathered him up in her arms, cuddling
him against her.

She was so tired. She wanted to rest for a few minutes
and she was hungry and thirsty. But she had to get the
baby to his mother.

He started to fret and Emily looked around the
kitchen. There were some pans on the floor, but there
wasn't as much damage as in her own kitchen. A pile of
diapers was stacked on the table and beside them stood a

baby bottle full of milk.

The milk's cold but maybe the baby won't mind, thought Emily. She didn't dare take time to heat it. He didn't mind. Emily settled herself in the big rocking chair by the stove. A small fire still smouldered in it and the pipes were still up. The baby sucked greedily at the bottle as he lay in her arms.

Emily dozed for a while and awoke with a start as the empty bottle fell to the floor. The baby was asleep, his long lashes making little black fans against his pink cheeks. She stroked his face with her finger.

She had to get moving again. There was no time to waste. She felt like staying in the house and waiting for Mrs. Howard to come but she couldn't. If that man was right, the town was going to blow up any minute. The other side of the mountain, away from the plant would be safer. And she still had to find Aunt Carrie.

Emily found a bun in the pantry and munched it as she refilled the bottle. Then she wrapped the baby in the shawls she found on the table. As she wrapped she tucked in a few diapers and the bottle too. Last of all she folded the white blanket with the blue rabbits on it around the whole thing.

He looked like a little mummy from a picture book about Egypt. Emily sipped some water, put the baby over her shoulder and left the house.

There was no one about. The rain had stopped but the

shortcut up the mountain would be muddy and slippery. Still, she had to try it. There might not be time to go around the long way.

At first it was easy. The terrible red light in the sky made everything as light as day. But as she climbed it was harder to find a good footing. She had only one hand free to pull herself up the slippery spots.

The baby got heavier at every step. She was afraid he would slide out of her arms. She had to stop and rest every few minutes. Once she slipped in the mud and slid backward. Only a thick bush saved her from tumbling back down.

Cold drops of water splattered on the baby's face and he started to cry. Emily wiped his tiny face with a corner of the blanket.

"Hush now, Alex, we're almost there. Then we'll find your mother and you'll be—"

A blinding white ball of fire erupted from the plant and arced through the sky. Emily felt herself pushed against the earth. She closed her eyes, wrapped her arms around the baby and tried to shield him with her body.

Beneath her she felt the mountain move. There was a deafening roar. Dirt and pebbles rained around them. Then everything was still.

Emily was terrified. She was afraid to move, afraid to open her eyes. The baby stirred and started to cry. He was alive. She couldn't sit here all night. No matter what happened she had to get Alex to his mother.

She opened her eyes and nearly fainted. Part of the mountain had moved. The path she had been climbing was gone. At the bottom was a pile of earth, stones, trees, and brush.

Her slide backward into the bushes had saved their lives. The bushes clung to an outcrop of rock. It had stayed solid when the explosion swept part of the mountain down to the street below.

She was afraid to move. If she did they might both go tumbling to the bottom. The baby squirmed and fretted and she knew she had to move. It was like a hideous nightmare.

Nightmare! She had dreamed this! The blue and white bundle that cried...the pink haze...the fall. No, she mustn't fall. Tom had said she could do anything she set her mind to.

Emily gritted her teeth. She was going to get this baby to safety. Far above her she could see the tip of the old cannon. It made her feel better to know it was still there.

Keeping her eyes on the cannon she moved Alex to her other shoulder and began to climb. Sometimes the earth shifted under her feet. Pebbles rattled down the slope onto her head.

As she climbed she heard shouts and stopped to look up. People were crowded near the cannon, looking down at what was left of the mountainside. They waved at her.

Emily was exhausted. Her arms ached. I've no breath left, she thought. I can't make it. But she had to go on. Another blast might sweep them away.

At last she reached the top. Hands reached down to help her up the last few feet.

A man tried to take the baby from her but she refused to give him up.

"It's Mrs. Howard's baby. I have to find her."

"She's down near the school, Emily, carrying on something fierce. I'll take you down. You're lucky to be alive, Miss. We thought the whole mountain was going to go but this side's all right."

Emily recognized the man from the Post Office. He took her arm and helped her stumble down through the crowds of people.

Mrs. Howard sat wrapped in blankets under a tree. She rocked back and forth with her hands over her face.

"My baby," she moaned. "Where's my baby?"

Emily collapsed on the ground beside her and put Alex in her lap. "Here he is, Mrs. Howard, I found him in the house."

She didn't remember much after that. People fussed around her. Someone covered her with a blanket. She curled up and fell asleep right there on the ground.

The next thing she knew another explosion sent pillars

of fire into the sky and she was wide awake. Cries and moans filled the air. People began to sing "Rock of Ages".

Emily sat up and put her head on her knees. She was cold and hungry and tired. It seemed like days since they had eaten Thanksgiving dinner, but she knew it was still the same day. Would it never end?

She hoped Mama was safe at the farm, but where was Aunt Carrie? She couldn't stay here doing nothing. She had to find her.

Emily stood up and folded the blanket.

"Where are you going, Emily?" Mrs. Howard shifted the baby from one arm to the other. "You didn't sleep long. You must still be tired out. How you dragged my poor baby up that mountain with it falling apart right under you, I'll never know. I'll always be in your debt." She started to cry.

"I gave Ruby a piece of my mind for forgetting the baby. Sent her right back after him, I did. And when she comes back I'll give her another piece of my mind."

"I feel better now, Mrs. Howard. I have to look for Aunt Carrie. We don't know where she went after the plant blew up."

"Well here. Take my wool shawl. Your jacket's damp. Mustn't catch cold, though it won't matter much. We're all doomed."

Emily shivered and wrapped the shawl around her shoulders. She searched among the people gathered on the mountainside. She could recognize faces even though it was night. The weird glow from the fiery munitions plant lit up the sky for miles around.

There was no sign of Aunt Carrie and no one had seen her. Emily tried to think. Where would she have gone? Maybe she went to the dairy where she used to work. It was worth a try.

Emily went past the school with its doors gaping, and down the hill toward Dundas Street where all the shops were. When she reached it, she stopped and stared.

Signs hung crookedly. Doors were flung wide or lay in the street, torn from their hinges. Broken glass glistened in the eerie light from the sky. Clothing and goods from the window displays were strewn over the road.

Emily was afraid. It was spooky. The Post Office clock said midnight, but the terrible red light from the munitions plant lit the whole town. She didn't want to walk down that long empty street to the dairy. What if there was another explosion from the plant?

But I've got to find Aunt Carrie, she thought. She needs someone to look after her. And Tom. Where was he? And Uncle Bert. Did he die in the explosion? Emily shivered and tightened the shawl around her. She didn't dare think. It was better to do something.

She picked her way carefully through the broken glass. It felt strange to be walking right down the middle of the street and not have to worry about horses and buggies and autos.

Emily was almost to the Post Office when she heard voices. She crouched between the steps and the wall making herself as small as possible.

Across the street three figures ran out of the cigar store. They carried boxes and darted out of sight between the buildings. Emily waited and watched.

Soon one of the figures came back out and crossed the corner to the bakery. It was a boy and he looked familiar. Dooley Smith! Emily couldn't be sure but the old fear welled up inside her.

She didn't want Dooley to see her. She had defied him once but her courage was gone. She had used it all up climbing the mountain with the Howard baby.

Emily rose. She was getting out of there. Whatever he was doing inside that store was none of her business. She had to find Aunt Carrie.

Crash! Emily froze.

The noise came from the bakery where Dooley was. It wasn't an explosion. Then she heard a thin wail, like a baby crying.

Emily wanted to hurry on. Whatever had happened to Dooley Smith, she didn't care. Let him look after himself. She took three steps, then stopped.

He must be in trouble. Maybe he was badly hurt. She couldn't just leave him there. There was no one around to help. After the crash she'd heard footsteps running away down the alley. His friends had run when they heard the crash. Some friends.

Emily crossed the street and peered into the shadows beyond the doorway. Cookies and buns and cakes were scattered all over the place. Shelves of bread had fallen and pushed over the counter.

"Help!...please...help."

Emily saw a big black boot sticking out.

Stepping carefully, she looked over the top of the counter.

Dooley Smith was flat on his back, covered with loaves of bread. On top of his leg, rested the huge brass cash register.

"Ooooh...Em'ly...get help...ooooh...it hurts...hurry!" His face twisted in pain as he stared up at her. "I can't move my leg."

Emily stared at him. "What are you doing in here, Dooley Smith?"

"Never you mind. Just get me some help. Do as I say or I'll get you."

The old fear of him came rushing back. What if he managed to push off the cash register and chase her? She thought of all the times he had chased her 'til she was out of breath and had a pain in her chest.

She should leave him there for someone else to find, but she knew that wasn't right. She had to try to help him even though she hated him.

Emily tugged at the cash register but it was too heavy. Its drawer was open and money had tumbled out all over Dooley and the floor. That's what he'd been after.

Dooley pushed himself up on his elbows and watched her. His face was pale and glistening with sweat. Each time she pushed he moaned. Finally he sank back and closed his eyes.

He's fainted, thought Emily. I'll have to find someone else to help him. I can't do this by myself.

She stood up and Dooley opened his eyes. "Don't go, Em'ly. Please...help me."

"I can't Dooley. I'll have to get help. I'm looking for Aunt Carrie but the first person I see I'll tell them about you."

"I saw your crazy aunt. Honest I did. If you get help, I'll tell you where she is."

Emily crouched beside him. "Where, Dooley, where is she? Tell me."

Dooley lay back and closed his eyes. He shook his head. "Not till you get help, Em'ly."

CHAPTER NINE

E**MILY STOOD THERE** for a moment wondering what to do. She had to find someone. Dooley wouldn't tell her about Aunt Carrie until she did. She would have helped him anyway, but he wouldn't believe her.

She darted back to the street. It was still deserted. Then she heard the tramp of heavy boots from the direction of the bridge. Soldiers in khaki uniforms marched toward her. They broke ranks in the middle of the street and Emily ran to the nearest one.

"Help," she cried. "Dooley needs help."

She pointed toward the bake shop and followed the soldier as he ran.

"Well, guess you caught yourself a looter, little lady." The soldier grinned at her as he knelt beside Dooley.

"That's what we're here for—to prevent looting. Now let's get this thing off your leg young man."

Dooley groaned as the soldier lifted the cash register off his leg.

"Have to get a stretcher. This leg looks bad," he said to Emily. "Be right back."

Emily bent over Dooley.

"Where is she? Where's Aunt Carrie?"

Dooley opened his eyes. "At the plant, Em'ly. I went up there and I saw her near the gate."

Emily started to go then turned back. "My name is Emily, Dooley Smith, not Em'ly."

But there was no answer. Dooley had fainted.

Emily ran across the bridge and followed the street up the other side of the river. She ran as if Dooley Smith were after her and her thoughts raced with her feet.

Why had Aunt Carrie gone to the plant? She must be in terrible danger. Emily had lost count of the explosions.

Soon the plant came in sight. She could feel the heat of the fires that raged through it. A group of people clustered around the gate, kept back by soldiers. Some of them had blackened clothing and burns. They must be workers who escaped, thought Emily. Maybe Uncle Bert and Tom were there.

She searched the crowd, covering her face with Mrs. Howard's shawl to keep out the searing smell of burning chemicals. Her aunt was not there. Neither were her uncle or cousin. She was tired and hungry. One of those buns that covered Dooley would taste good right now. She was thirsty, too.

Emily left the crowd and walked down to the river. She would get a drink there and wash her hot face. She climbed out on the rocks and dipped her hands into the water. It was cool and refreshing. She dried herself on the shawl and turned to climb back up to the street.

Up to the left was a pile of rocks left by the diggers when they built the plant. At the top, silhouetted against the fiery sky, stood a tall, thin woman in a pale dress. Her arms were rigid at her sides as she stared into the blazing inferno. She began to walk slowly toward the fires.

"Aunt Carrie!" screamed Emily.

Emily scrambled up the slope screaming her name all the way, but her aunt kept moving toward the flames. Her beautiful red hair swirled around her shoulders, glinting in the light of the flames devouring the buildings.

Her face was the saddest Emily had ever seen. Tears made streaks through black, sooty smudges on her cheeks.

Emily grabbed her hand in both of hers. She had to get her away from the fire. Then a wonderful thing happened. Aunt Carrie stopped and looked at her. Really looked at her. She hadn't really looked at anyone in a long time.

"It's done, Emily." She looked back into the flames. "The evil place has gone."

"Let's go home, Aunt Carrie."

Emily led her away. As they left the heat of the inferno Aunt Carrie shivered.

"Here, Aunt Carrie, take this shawl. My coat's dry now. Your dress is so thin."

Her aunt wrapped it around her shoulders. "Silly me, to come out in a summer dress."

They walked in silence for a while then she spoke again.

"Why would I do that, Emily, put on a summer dress this time of year?" She looked around at the bare branches of the trees and the piles of leaves on the ground.

Emily didn't know what to say. How could she tell her aunt she hadn't been in her right mind for two months?

They crossed the bridge and turned down Front Street, stepping carefully over the broken glass. When they came to the dairy where Aunt Carrie had worked she stopped and stared at it.

"Where's my hat, Emily, my wedding hat?"

"It's..." Emily's mind raced. Where was that hat? She remembered Tom standing on the porch with it in his hand, but then where had it gone? So much had happened since that first explosion. It seemed years ago but it had only been last night.

"It's at home," Aunt Carrie.

I hope it is anyway, thought Emily. What if someone had stolen it? The doors were blown open and there wasn't a pane of glass in any window. Someone could have walked in and taken it, but most people had left town. Looters wouldn't want a hat anyway. Emily pulled her away.

"Come on, let's go home and look for it."

There were more people on the streets now. There hadn't been a blast for some time. They had left the mountain and were going back to their homes, hoping that the horror was over. Houses were still standing but there wasn't a single pane of glass in any of them.

Ahead of her Emily saw Mrs. Howard carrying baby Alex. Ruby walked behind, pushing the baby carriage full of their belongings. She doesn't look beautiful now, thought Emily. Ruby's golden hair no longer shone. It was dull and stringy. Her face was dirty and she had slept in her clothes. She looked cross.

Emily couldn't help feeling glad that Ruby didn't look beautiful all the time. She knew she didn't look any better herself. Her clothes and face and hands were filthy, and her hair frizzed around her head like a halo. She'd lost her hair ribbon somewhere on the mountain but she didn't care.

Emily slowed down. She didn't want to catch up with Mrs. Howard and Ruby. She didn't feel like talking to anyone. She was cold and tired and hungry and she just wanted to go home.

She put her hand in her pocket then remembered that Muff was gone. Never again would she feel his comforting piggy shape. That made her think of Pa too. She hadn't had time to think of Muff or Pa since the plant blew up. There'd been too much to do.

Her thoughts whirled. Was Mama all right? Where were Tom and Uncle Bert? Maybe they had tried to go back home again. Was Aunt Carrie going to be all right now?

They found the house empty. Aunt Carrie paid no attention to the mess of glass and fallen plaster but went looking for her hat.

"Here it is!" she said, snatching it off the phonograph. She smoothed the flowers with her fingers and wrapped the trailing lace around the crown. "It was going to be the most beautiful wedding hat in all of Trenton."

Her voice was sad and dreamy. Emily was afraid she was going back into her former state but she didn't. She hugged the hat to her for a moment then put it back on the phonograph.

"I'll change my clothes, then we have to get this place cleaned up. You find something to put all this glass in."

She went upstairs and Emily ran to look in the wood-shed. She felt relieved. Aunt Carrie seemed normal again and it was good to be doing something. She found cardboard boxes and a basket and took them into the kitchen.

Her aunt came down wearing a blue checked house dress and a huge apron. She had combed her hair and put it up and washed her hands and face.

"Now Emily let's get started on the kitchen first. We'd better find some old gloves to handle all this glass."

She got a shovel and started scooping it up. "While we're working you can tell me everything that's happened since I've been...away."

So Emily told her about Uncle Bert and Tom coming to live with them, about the explosions, about her mother having the 'flu and escaping to Uncle Bert's farm, and about finding the baby in the Howard house. She didn't mention the boarders leaving because of Aunt Carrie's noise at night.

They dragged the boxes of glass out to the shed, then stopped for a rest. Daylight was lightening the sky though it was still red from the fires.

"A cup of tea would be nice," said Aunt Carrie.

"We can't make a fire. The stovepipe is down," said Emily.

"Well, there's lots of water in the well. We can drink that. Let's raid the pantry and see what we can find. We can pretend we're on a treasure hunt and the treasure is food."

Emily giggled. Trust Aunt Carrie to make a game of it. It was almost like old times, but there was a strange sadness about her.

They found bread and jam and cheese and piled their plates. Aunt Carrie filled cups from the water pail and they sat down at the table and dived into their food.

The last food Emily had eaten was the bun she'd found in Mrs. Howard's kitchen. She remembered Dooley stretched out on the floor of the bakery, covered with bread and buns. Too bad she hadn't put one in her pocket.

When the last crumb was gone Aunt Carrie smiled at her.

"I guess I haven't been much help to you and your mother, Emily. I'm sorry. I'll try to make it up to you."

She rubbed her forehead. "It all seems like a dream. I remember the men telling me that Robert was dead and then..."

Her voice trembled and she wiped her eyes.

"The next thing I knew I was jolted out of my chair on the porch and balls of fire lit up the sky. That wicked place had blown up." She covered her face with her hands.

"Why did you go to the plant, Aunt Carrie?" Emily asked. "Tom and I didn't know where you'd gone."

"I thought Robert was still alive and in the fire. I ran all the way. I watched that terrible fire and then I remembered he was dead. I wanted to walk into the fire and be with him."

She reached over and took Emily's hand. "Then you came, Emily. I was so glad to see you. I knew I didn't want to die..." Her voice trailed off and she stared at the doorway.

Emily turned and saw two blackened shapes appear in the opening.

"Tom! Bert!" Emily and Aunt Carrie shrieked together.

The two sagged against the doorway, without speaking. Emily and her aunt helped them over to the couch.

"We're fine...awful tired...hungry," Uncle Bert said weakly.

Tom leaned his head against the wall and closed his eyes. "Water," he mumbled, "dying." He started to shake.

Emily ran to get a dipperful of water. "Oh Tom, here. Try to take a sip."

Then she realized Tom was shaking with laughter.

"Oh Emily, you should see your face. Thought I was dying didn't you? You're so funny."

Emily poured the water over his head. "Who's funny now, Tom Rogers. You should see *your* face."

Tom sputtered and wiped his face with his sleeve, leaving long pale streaks in the soot.

"Aw, can't you take a joke? Gee, Emily, don't cry. I was just having some fun."

Emily threw the dipper down beside him. "I'm not crying. I'm through crying. If you want water get it yourself."

Tom moaned and pretended to collapse, but Emily left him to help her aunt get more food.

They all sat around the table while Tom and his father ate and told about their night of terror.

"I was just finishing my shift when the whistle blew," Uncle Bert said as he munched leftover turkey. "I stayed to find out what was happening.

"Somebody said an acid mixture went wrong and boiled over, and set fire to the wooden struts under the vats. The fire was spreading. I knew right away we were in trouble."

He stopped to gulp some milk.

"We knew when the fire reached the guncotton and the TNT, the whole plant would blow up."

Uncle Bert took his pipe out of his pocket and lit a match. Then he blew it out and put the pipe away. "Don't want to see any more fire for a while. Even a match," he said.

"The siren went and we were told to run for our lives. The place was going to go up. There were two box cars full of TNT on the siding. When the fire reached that it would be goodbye Trenton."

Emily shuddered and Aunt Carrie hugged her close. It was all over, but she felt more afraid now than she had during the whole terrible night.

"Go on, Dad, what happened then?" Tom urged.

"Some of us volunteered to stay. We hacked away at the trestles leading to the acid tanks and the TNT. It was time enough for one of the engineers to chug his engine in and pull the box cars away. There was so much smoke it's a wonder he could see. He's a brave man.

"Then we were ordered to leave...just in time. The first explosion knocked me over as I got to the gate. Some of the roofs on nearby houses caught fire from the debris so I stayed to help them out. Next thing I knew there was Tom beside me, helping."

Tom broke in. "Yup, I couldn't see anything for smoke and flames and people. I looked all over for you, Dad."

His father leaned over and squeezed his shoulder. "You did well, Tom. I'm proud of you."

Tom's chest swelled. "Gee, Dad, thanks I—"

BOOM!

Chapter Ten

THEY CROUCHED WHERE they were, covering their heads with their arms. The whole house shuddered and more plaster fell from the ceiling. There were no window panes left to shatter.

For a moment there was that terrible silence that followed every blast. Emily raised her head. Tom stared at her, his face white.

"That's the last time I open my mouth," he whispered trying to keep his lips together. "Every time I do, something blows up."

Emily couldn't help but giggle. "You're powerful, Tom, you are."

By this time there were noises from the street and they all went outside to see what was happening. People were poking their heads out of what was left of their doors and windows.

A man came tearing down the street, knees pumping, followed by his wife and a child. He stopped for breath in front of Uncle Bert.

"Run! Run for your life, folks!" he panted. "'Nother explosion any minute. Trenton's going sky high."

He grabbed his family and tore down the street.

Emily sat down on the porch steps and folded her arms. "I'm not going anywhere. I'm staying right here. I'm tired of running. I'm never going to run again...ever!"

Uncle Bert smiled. "Good for you, Emily. I don't think there'll be any more blasts. Anyway, I'm not budging either."

"I think we all need a sleep," said Aunt Carrie. "It's been a long night. Let's have a rest then we can decide what to do."

Emily lay down on her bed and pulled the quilt over her. She closed her eyes. She'd never been so tired in her life. But sleep wouldn't come. She kept thinking of all the things that had happened since last evening—the explosion, baby Alex, Dooley, and Aunt Carrie.

She put her hand under her pillow. Then she remembered. Muff wasn't there. How could she ever go to sleep without Muff? She must write to Pa and tell him every-thing that had happened. Now she had something to write about. He'd never believe it. As soon as she got up...

Two hours later the sun streaming in the window woke Emily. She washed and changed her clothes and went down to the warm kitchen. Aunt Carrie was sitting at the table with a cup of tea. The stove and the stovepipe were back in place, and Emily could smell porridge.

"Have some breakfast, Emily. Bert's gone to the Post Office to see what's happening. Tom's walking to Wooler to bring back your mother, and you and I can start getting this place cleaned up."

It felt good to be busy. Uncle Bert came back to report that the whole plant had burned down, but not a single person had been killed.

"That's a miracle," said Aunt Carrie. "Did you bring any glass for the windows?"

"Not a sheet of glass to be had. I went to every hard-ware store in Trenton. A load of glass is coming up from Belleville this afternoon. Tom and I'll get at the windows as soon as we get the glass."

Emily heard the jingle of harness and the clip-clop of the horse's hooves before anyone else. She rushed out to the wagon to hug her mother. She was still weak but looked better.

"I was so worried about you all," she said. "We could

see the light in the sky and hear the explosions even at Wooler."

They all helped unload bundles and get Beth Rogers into the house. Mrs. Jackson and her family went across the street to their own house, and Tom took the horse and wagon away.

At dinner her mother made Emily tell everything that had happened after she had been loaded on the wagon and sent out of town.

In the middle of her story Emily looked at Tom. "Where did you get that horse, Tom? Who does he belong to?"

Tom grinned and shook his hair out of his eyes. "Mr. Baker up the street asked me to feed his horse while he took his family to Toronto for a few days. I didn't think he'd mind if I borrowed the horse and wagon. It was sort of an emergency."

"I guess it was. You've got a good head on your shoulders, Tom." Uncle Bert winked at his son.

Tom blushed and hung his head. Emily poked him.

"Admiring your boots, Tom?"

"Aw go on, Emily, I—" He broke off as a large shadow darkened the doorway.

A tall man with a bushy black beard stood there. He looked around the room for a moment then pointed at Emily.

"If you're Em'ly Rogers, my son, Dooley, wants to

speak to you. He's out in the auto. Can't come in. Darn fool broke his leg last night getting into trouble. That'll teach him a lesson he'll never forget."

Emily blinked. She'd almost forgotten about Dooley. She really didn't want to see him.

"I'll be mighty pleased if you'll come, Miss. Dooley's caused a lot of trouble, but he's promised to turn over a new leaf. Might as well start today, I said. So here we are."

Tom took her arm. "I'll come with you, Emily. Don't be afraid."

Emily yanked her arm away and put her chin in the air. "I'm not afraid. You can come if you like but I'm not afraid."

She marched out to the big grey auto parked at the curb. Dooley didn't look very frightening. He was pale and was stretched out in the back seat. His leg was in a cast and he was holding a crutch.

He put his hand in his pocket. "Guess this belongs to you, Em-i-ly. I found it after you tripped me the other day. Can't see why you set such a store by an old stone pig."

His father growled and Dooley handed Muff over to Emily.

Emily was thrilled. She almost liked Dooley at that moment. She hugged Muff. "Thank you."

Then she remembered all the times he had chased her

home and her heart hardened.

"Why do you always chase me home, Dooley?"

Dooley grinned his old wicked grin. "It was fun teasing you, Em'ly. All I had to do was look at you to make you run. You scare so easy, I couldn't help it."

His father growled again and Dooley went on. "Anyway, I'm sorry. I wanted to find that missing money too. I looked for it every time I chased you home."

He waved his hand and grinned as his father drove away.

Emily tucked Muff into her pocket, and she and Tom went back to the house.

"I don't think he's one bit sorry," said Tom.

"I don't think he is either but it doesn't matter. I won't ever run away from him again—no matter what he does."

Tom stopped by the porch and kicked the leaves around. "I wonder where that pay packet went. It's a real mystery."

"Oh the wind probably blew it off the table," said Emily. "Aunt Carrie put it down beside her hat when she came home. It was windy that day."

She stopped. If Aunt Carrie was afraid the wind would blow it away, what did she do with it? Put it in something, under something? Maybe she hid it. She liked to tease Robert, her fiancé...but where? The hat, the big straw wedding hat with all the flowers and lace decorating it...

Emily grabbed Tom's hand and raced into the house, through the kitchen into the parlour. The hat was still on the phonograph.

She took it to Aunt Carrie in the kitchen. "Tom, get Aunt Carrie's sewing basket, quick!"

Tom put it on the table beside the hat.

"Now, Aunt Carrie, would you take all the decorations off that hat?"

"Emily!" her mother's voice was shocked.

"Please. It's important," Emily begged.

Aunt Carrie took her scissors out of her sewing box and started to snip. First the veiling came off, then the flowers. Soon all that was left was the wide yellow band around the crown.

"Look!" shouted Tom.

They all saw it—the corner of a brown packet poking out from underneath the band. Aunt Carrie plucked it out, then burst into tears.

"I remember now. I wanted to tease Robert. Wanted him to hunt for the surprise. Then he never came...and I forgot."

Beth Rogers put her arms around her sister and nodded at the others. "Can't you find something to do? I'll look after Carrie. Go and do something useful."

Uncle Bert went downtown to see if the glass had arrived, and Tom began work on the woodshed door. Emily curled her fingers around Muff in her pocket and

walked to the end of the street. The mountain looked different now—parts of it sheared off by the blasts. There was nothing left of the path but someone would start a new one soon. It was a good shortcut to school.

She stared up at the place where she had crouched with baby Alex. It was all like a dream, but now maybe Mrs. Howard would let her look after him sometimes.

Emily was almost at the house when she saw the telegraph boy coming down the street. He stopped in front of her house, leaned his bike against a tree and went to the door.

She never knew how she got there so fast, but Emily was in the kitchen before the boy had time to get back to his bike.

Aunt Carrie stood by the stove, her eyes wide, hands pressed to her mouth. Tom stared from the shed door. Her mother sat at the table, staring at the yellow envelope in her hand.

"Mama?" Emily could barely speak.

Her mother put the telegram on the table and buried her head in her arms.

"I can't open it. I won't."

Emily stared at it for a few seconds, then grabbed the envelope and ripped it open with shaking fingers.

Her eyes scanned the words.

She couldn't believe it.

"Mama!" she grabbed her mother. "Pa isn't dead. He's wounded. He's coming home—soon!"

Beth Rogers read the telegram herself. "Oh it's true. It's true. He's coming home! Thank God!"

Everybody started to cry. Even Tom had tears in his eyes.

"Hey, Emily," he said. "It's good news. Why is everybody crying? I thought you weren't ever going to cry again."

Emily looked at him as if he wasn't very bright. "It's all right to cry now, Tom. Everything's all right. Call me a fountain if you like, but I'm going to have a good cry."

And she did.